THE HIDDEN LANGUAGE OF DEMONS

Books by L.H. Maynard & M.P.N. Sims

Shadows at Midnight
Echoes of Darkness
Incantations
The Hidden Language of Demons
Moths
The Secret Geography of Nightmare
Selling Dark Miracles

As editors

Cold Touch
Darkness Rising
Enigmatic Tales volumes 1-10
Enigmatic Novellas volumes 1-6
Enigmatic Variations volumes 1-5
Enigmatic Electronic online
Best Of Enigmatic Tales
F20

THE HIDDEN LANGUAGE OF DEMONS

LH MAYNARD & MPN SIMS

PRIME BOOKS

The Hidden Language of Demons

www.primebooks.net

ISBN: 1-894815-13-0

For our children - Iain Maynard & Emily Sims

THE HIDDEN LANGUAGE OF DEMONS

One split into two became three, and the world spun on, but not as we know it, and nevermore became today, with yesterday little more than a song, and a future mapped out like madness from the mountain, with extra pepperoni.

Two motorcycles skidded to a halt at a wire fence, and the dust they threw up into the still morning air hung motionless like a cloud in the otherwise blue sky, a mute calling card of their arrival. Behind them the land was flat, expressionless as if someone had ironed out all the creases, the black snake road they had travelled the only real distinguishing feature amongst mile after mile of desert sand and rock.

Through the wire they could see buildings strung out like a low level mini city, with sentry posts, dogs on chains, military vehicles, locked doors stamped with 'No Entry', CCTV cameras trained on them, but they couldn't see any people. One of the riders looked at his watch and glanced at his companion. They both lifted the black visors of their helmets and impassively surveyed the familiar defences in front of them. They had only been gone a few days, and already the compound seemed alien to them.

Apart from the snarling dogs, chained on long leads, there didn't seem to be any sign of life. The second rider kept one hand on the leather holster at his hip, actively watching for danger, his eyes expression free, like the land behind and around him. He spoke to the other rider for a moment and they both smiled, their eyes remaining cold, and one of them nodded.

They both leant on their siren horns, the sudden noise rending the silence, echoing away into the heat of the early morning like the cry of a wounded beast.

The two riders were riding escort for a silver grey limousine; the man inside opened the rear window and leaned his head out. "Will you two clowns shut the hell up? Use your radio to call the sentry; it's just after six in the morning. Do you want to wake the whole centre?"

Walt Whitney left the window open despite the already oppressive heat outside, and listened to the traces of the motor horns echoing away into the distance where the sand dunes would swallow them before they crashed into the mountain range on the horizon. He watched as the haze began to rise from the black tarmac of the road, knowing from his years here that it would bubble up by midday, and subside again as the cold of the evening crept up on them all.

The gates opened, armed guards very much in evidence now, and the limousine moved gently forwards, driving round to the side entrance of the main complex building, where Whitney had his office. As Director of the unnamed, secret research centre located anonymously in the Nevada deserts, his job was to gain and maintain funding both from the Government and from the private sector. He had just returned from a trip to Washington to put his budget proposals for the forthcoming year before the committee of generals, administrators and politicians who comprised his paymasters

It had been a tough and gruelling assignment. If he had known what lay ahead in the coming days for him, his staff, and others within and without the centre, he would have considered the task just completed a holiday by comparison.

⁂

Days went past and still the question waited to be asked. It wasn't through indecision, more a lack of opportunity. The question had to be asked before he would get a response. He knew he wanted to ask it, knew he was certain what he wanted her answer to be. He wanted to marry Imogen and he wanted to ask her tonight.

Their favourite restaurant in Boston had taken his reservation over a week ago, and he had spent the time since then mentally rehearsing what he would say to her. He was sure she would say yes, but he wanted to have a clear conscience about it. The fact that she was the only daughter of his boss was an added complication, at least in his mind.

The meal was wonderful, even though Daniel Parker nervously drank too much wine.

The wine waiter lingered by their table. "Another bottle of the Vouvray, sir?"

"Yes, why not?" Daniel said, and the man rushed away delighted by this response, as though a personal compliment had been paid to him. Daniel could only hope Imogen's delight was as great in reply to his question.

For the moment she looked annoyed. "Don't you think we've had enough wine, Daniel?"

It is turning into a night for questions, Daniel thought, and realised he was getting drunk. "What you mean is *I've* had enough wine, and yes, you're probably right. But then I'm nervous."

Imogen flicked back a lock of her blonde hair and smiled, if a little uncertainly. "Can I guess what you're nervous about?"

"No," he said, as the wine cork was extracted and the second bottle poured into their glasses. "I've had enough of questions, with one exception." He pushed his chair back, and dropped to one knee beside her. "Imogen, I love you, and I want to marry you. Will you marry me?"

Her reply was delayed by a burst of applause from some of the other diners who turned collectively to look at

Imogen, anxious for the right answer. Daniel smiled shyly and looked at her as well. Imogen sipped her wine, and a worm of doubt began to creep into the room. "I've been hoping you'd ask that for weeks, and I know what my answer will be, but I'm not going to give it to you tonight. You've drunk too much, and this is too public a place."

The other diners shrugged in mutual embarrassment and went back to their meals. Daniel sat back onto his chair while Imogen called for the bill. They avoided each other's eyes while they paid for the meal and put on their coats.

It was starting to rain as they went out into the cold night air, and a sudden flash of lightning made Imogen jump with fright. Instinctively, Daniel drew her into him. She wriggled in his arms until she was facing him. "Of course I'll marry you," she said quietly. When he squeezed her she thought she would never be able to breathe again.

Not far away a sleek black stretch limo eased itself from the kerb, tyres whirring on the rain soaked street. It glided almost noiselessly, its engine purring softly like a contented cat. From behind its heavily tinted windows four pairs of eyes watched Imogen and Daniel as they walked. The minds behind the eyes were speculative but confident.

Thunder boomed overhead in counterpoint to the crackling lightning, as the rain grew more insistent. It was late and all the shops were closed, the restaurants and pubs silent. The buildings either side of them loomed large and empty, the street was cold and desolate.

"It's a little eerie when it's all shut down like this," Imogen said.

Daniel pulled her closer to him. "It's just the storm." He couldn't think any bad thoughts tonight.

Imogen was quickening her pace, pulling on his arm. "You would expect to see someone though, there's no-one about."

The long black car cruised past them in the opposite direction, doing about twenty miles an hour, headlights off, its driver hidden behind the tinted glass. As it passed them it slowed perceptively.

"There," Daniel said. "Satisfied?"

"Looks like a hearse."

Daniel ignored her and pointed. "We'll cut across the new plaza, it's quicker."

At the end of the street the car performed a silent turn until at first it was facing them, and then following them.

The shopping plaza was to their right, a wide expanse of new pink flagstones, the central area a huge pedestrian precinct boarded on three sides by glass fronted shops and offices. It was decorated in concrete, with fountains and towering modern statues. The fountains were dormant at night, although the rain gave water enough to compensate. It was when they passed one of the statues, a poorly realised effigy of a man riding a cubist horse, for the second time, that Daniel knew he was lost.

"Daniel, please don't do this, I'm frightened enough already." As she spoke a loud rumble of thunder seemed to shake the statue into movement. She looked behind her but she couldn't see anyone or anything there. The storm was getting worse.

The blaze of headlights blinded them suddenly, as the car emerged from a road opposite. It rolled silently and smoothly into the precinct and stopped, sideways on to them, a hundred yards away.

"How did they manage that?" Daniel said, almost to himself.

One window slid down and an arm reached out from within; a long slim arm, naked but for a diamond bracelet that glittered in the moonlight. In the elegant hand was a cocktail glass, an olive floating in the crystal clear liquid of the drink.

"Daniel, I don't like this," Imogen said.

Daniel disengaged his arm from hers. "Relax, they've probably been to a party or something. I'll see what they want."

She grabbed at his sleeve. "No, that's not what this is about. People coming home from parties don't go out of their way to terrorise total strangers."

Daniel turned to her and sighed. "No one's being terrorised. Wait here." He took her hand from his sleeve, and started walking towards the car.

The arm from the window remained motionless. As Daniel walked to the car he could see the rain ripple the surface of the drink. The car's engine was nothing more than a steady beat, throbbing in time to the swish of the wipers across the wet windscreen. There was the sound of muffled laughter from inside the car, and he thought he was right about them being partygoers.

Daniel was at the door of the car when Imogen called out to him. He turned towards her, and in that moment the arm moved. The slim hand smashed the glass against the side of the car and brought the stem slicing up towards his face. He was caught off balance as the jagged glass ripped into his cheek. He reeled away but the white-hot pain in his cheek stayed with him. The car door opened, slamming against his legs, pitching him to the ground. Then the door slammed shut and the car's engine roared like a demented beast. Daniel tried to scrabble to his feet, convinced they were going to run him over, but the car drove past him, and he knew where it was heading.

"Run, Imogen!" he shouted. Shakily he stood, and started to follow the car.

Imogen was paralysed with fear. She was crying, weeping large tears that mingled with the rain on her face. As the car reached her, a taloned hand pushed out from inside and grabbed her wrist. Another claw planted itself in her hair, twisting cruelly, yanking her towards the open window. Yet another made a grab at her coat, and she heard the material rip. The paralysis left her, and she began to struggle, but there were too many of them. She was making small frightened noises in the back of her throat as she fought to be free, but her strength was ebbing away. Her body was lifted like a rag doll into the air and pulled effortlessly into the pitch-black interior of the car. It was only then that she screamed.

Daniel stumbled across the precinct, slipping on the rain-wet flagstones. The car was still there, engine idling, making no attempt to move off. It sat there mocking him, making him feel useless and guilty, guilty for not listening to Imogen.

Imogen screamed again, but the scream was cut dead. Silence fell over the precinct, even the car's engine had died. Daniel stopped a few yards from the car, his breathing ragged. He shielded his eyes from the glare of the headlights as his mind sought frantic solutions.

All four doors of the car swung open and four women stepped out from the gloomy interior. Four stunningly beautiful women, wearing expensive, revealing, elegant evening dresses. Their perfectly made up faces looked the result of a high-class beauty parlour, and they wore their hair loose, flowing freely in reckless cascades. They came around to the front of the car and stood looking at Daniel.

Their beauty was only a facade. When he looked into the eyes of the women what he saw made him more frightened than ever. The eyes of the four were the same, pale blue, burning with cruelty and anger. He tore his gaze away from them and felt himself take a step backwards in an involuntary reflex movement. Blood trickled from the lips of one of the women, the one with hair like flames. The black haired one had her fist tightly clenched around a scrap of Imogen's coat. They all wore a look of hunger on their immaculately made up faces.

The blonde took a step towards him, and he turned and ran. The rain lashed into his face, thunder clapped in applause above, while lightning forked in illumination. He was conscious that the women were closing in on him, like wild animals for the kill. He glanced behind him and saw them, gliding towards him, oblivious to the storm, their dresses dry, flowing like a cool breeze around their bodies, their hair unnaturally perfect, not even windswept. Then he tripped and fell.

The women stood motionless, watching him now with curiously neutral expressions. Then one of them raised her arm, the same arm that had held the cocktail glass. The statue of the horseman began to move, horse rearing, rider leaning back in the saddle, pulling on the reins. The sound of bronze hooves clattering down on the wet granite plinth filled the night, rising above the howling storm, filling Daniel's head, forcing his hands up to cover his ears. The woman lowered her arm and the statue was motionless again.

The brown haired woman turned her head to look at the fountain, blinked her cold blue eyes and the fountain gushed into life, its spray climbing high into the air to join the rain. At its peak it vaporised, forming a mist that swirled around them. The woman blinked and the fountain shut down again.

The women moved in on him. Daniel had only one choice if they were not to finish him. As the blonde one took another step Daniel rushed at her, and knocked into her. She hissed, raking his face with her fingernails, but he'd caught her off balance and there was nothing she could do to stop him pushing past her. He was out of the circle of women and running. Behind him they cried out, howling in the night.

He had gained himself a few seconds, no more, and he couldn't even spare a moment to look back to see how close they were. He just ran, twisting and swerving through the rain swept precinct. As he ran the place came alive. Every fountain in the plaza threw up a spray into the night sky, clouding the air with their fine mist. Each of the statues breathed into life, the bizarre shaped figures peering down at him, helping the hunters catch their prey.

Daniel stopped, and ran in a different direction as one of the women appeared in the mist ahead of him. Three paces more and there was another one. He turned again and found himself face to face with the blonde. There was nowhere left to run, they had trapped him. They had steered him back to where he had started, as if they had been playing with him, turning him in circles.

Slowly out of the mist of the storm, meandering like snakes, they drew nearer. The facade of elegance and sophistication was abandoned, and they approached him in their true form. Faces ghostly white, their bodies crouched and tense. They were naked except for a few tattered rags draped around their filthy, emaciated bodies. Long wolfish tongues flicked over yellow, sharp teeth. He stared into their faces, looking for the beauty, and he saw only the hunger.

One of the women floated effortlessly into the air. A second joined her, levitating above Daniel, spitting and hissing at him. Then they fell on him, biting and clawing, ripping at his clothes, tearing at his hair. He tried to fight back, lashing out with his fists, grunting with satisfaction as his knuckles smashed into a woman's mouth, splintering her teeth. But they were too strong for him and he could feel himself blacking out, falling into an unconsciousness from which he knew there would be no return. In the sky above him lightning was flashing blood red and the wind was wailing.

Then the attack stopped. The women were gone.

His body in agony, Daniel staggered to his feet and stumbled hopelessly after them. Across the wet flagstones the women were racing back to the car. Its engine was roaring, doors flung open. The women fell into the car, slamming the doors shut behind them. The engine screamed, and the wheels spun briefly in the wet before it sped away.

"Imogen!" Daniel yelled.

From inside the car Imogen screamed, a scream of terror, and of insufferable pain. Something tiny was thrown from a rear window, before the car was lost in the rain and the darkness.

Daniel searched the puddles around his feet to find whatever it was they had thrown out. He found it. He sank to his knees, pressed his fists to his eyes, and began to sob.

It was Imogen's ring, the ruby ring he had given her on their first anniversary. The ring was still attached to her finger.

⁂

There was a gold star on the dressing room door, the interior of the room luxurious, with pine-clad walls, purple velvet drapes, low slung ceiling with concealed lighting. Against one wall an ox-blood leather Chesterfield, against the other a well stocked bar. Around the walls were framed photographs of famous comedy stars from stage and screen; Chaplin rubbing shoulders with Richard Pryor, Laurel and Hardy beaming across at Steve Martin.

On the dresser with the illuminated mirror stood two more framed photographs. One was of W C Fields, resplendent with straw hat and cane, the other was of a younger man, a man in his early forties with film star good looks, light brown hair just starting to turn grey at the temples. On a chain around his neck hung a 22 carat gold replica of a rolled-up one thousand dollar bill, and on his fingers were heavy gold rings. The man in the photograph was smiling, a curiously appealing smile that had the ability to draw people in and make them smile as well.

The two men in the photographs shared things in common. One was the name, one was they were both funny men. They weren't related although the younger man wouldn't discourage you from imagining they were; it was one of his hopes when he changed his natural name that people would think he was the son, possibly grandson of the famous W C.

That had been when Christopher Fielding was starting out on the road to comedy stardom, but now he had made it, or rather Chris Fields had; five nights headlining here at Las Vegas, as well as being the star of a top network TV show, and his last comedy album had gone platinum. A lot had happened to him in the intervening twenty or so years; ups and downs, getting booed off stage at small town strip joints, seeing his name in lights for the first time, relationships sacrificed. As he looked at the reflection in the mirror he saw the lines webbing out from the corners of his eyes, eyes that had long lost their boyish sparkle and that now were only dull, almost glazed.

There was a respectful tap at the door. "Five minutes, Mr Fields."

Five minutes and the sparkle had to be back in those eyes because it was Showtime and the customers who had paid their hard earned cash to watch his act would expect to see it there. He emptied the white powder into the centre of a small hand mirror, used a credit card to divide it into neat lines and then took the gold dollar bill from around his neck.

There was another knock at the door. "Curtain, Mr Fields."

The spotlight hit Fields in the eyes the moment he walked onto the stage. He put his hand up to shield them and made it look like a natural action in reaching for the microphone. The audience were applauding loudly, whistling happily in anticipation, almost drowning out the band, which was playing a medley of Frank Sinatra songs.

"Good evening, ladies and gentlemen," he said into the microphone. The audience quietened immediately, a few even laughed, and Fields said nothing more until they had all stopped. "No, don't stop, that's probably as good as it gets." The laughter started again, but the light was hurting his eyes.

He took the mike from its stand and began to pace about the stage but the light seemed to follow him, interrogating him almost. He launched into his act and before five minutes had passed the laughter was almost continuous. It rose and fell like a wave as the jokes and the stories hit their mark. He felt himself carried along on the tide of laughter, felt the fresh surge of adrenaline as he once again realised that the laughter and the applause had him hooked now as surely as the dreams of them had all those years ago. When it was like this it was easy, he could coast, it all took so little effort, he even had time to distance his mind and take in more of his surroundings.

The theatre was large, but low ceilinged, which gave an intimate atmosphere. The tables were crowded together and smoke hung in the air like grey gauze. His eyes settled onto a pretty blonde in the second row from the front. He directed his next gag to her and she rewarded him with a wet lipped smile full of promise. He'd keep her in mind for later.

He took out a silk handkerchief and wiped his brow. "Well, we've had some fun here tonight, but now, with your permission, I'd like to get a little serious." A stagehand brought out a high stool and Fields hoisted himself up onto it. "I'd like to talk about fear." The audience grew silent. "Yes, fear. It's something we all experience but rarely talk about, but I want to talk about it, with you, tonight." He was playing them along. Using his ability to play on an audience's reaction. It was an art he'd learned on his long haul to the top, and now he could work an audience, keeping them finely tuned. Knowing when to attack and when to treat them gently, coaxing them into seeing the funny line. He could feel the ripple travelling around the room now as he waited; they were not sure what was coming. "We all have fears. With some people it's the fear of flying, with others the fear of falling under a subway train." Someone laughed. "You think it's funny? You walk down any subway station and you can't miss them; they're the ones who look as if they've been nailed to the wall. Fear, it's a terrible thing and it affects us all. Even me, oh yes, I have to confess my fear to you, because I have a fear - Dentists." "Yeah." A voice in the audience called out. "Hey, you too? I thought it was just me, but then I guess not. A lot of people are scared of going to see their dentist. We can get together after the show; maybe get a little dialogue going, compare dental records. For me this fear started at an early age. I remember my mother getting me all dressed up – I looked cute in that sailor's suit – and she wouldn't tell me where we wee going. 'Where are we going, mummy?' 'You'll see when we get there.' That's all she'd say. 'You'll see when we get there.' Well, I knew that. When you get anywhere you know you're there. 'Are we going to the zoo?' 'You'll see when we get there.' The dentist was this old guy who had his surgery above a candy store, great for business. All the kids in the neighbourhood went to see him, and someone had told him that to make the kids feel safe he should do something, maybe wear something to reassure them. Except this man hated kids, really detested them. You walked into the surgery and the first thing you saw was the chair, and you'd seen a chair like that in the movies, and they were strapping a big bad man into it and then the lights flickered. The dentist himself looks about seventy, which he is, and he looks weird. He looks miserable as sin, but what really shuts you up is that on his head he's wearing this pair of Mickey Mouse ears. 'Siddown in the chair and shaddup.' "

Suddenly Fields felt a tightening in his temples, and a throbbing at the base of his skull. A party scene flashed into his brain. There were lights, and people laughing, drinks and food, dancing and . . .

"You can always tell when a dentist has been invited to a party. All the guests are having conversations with their mouths closed; it's like being at a ventriloquist's convention. The hostess wanders over to you arm in arm with some guy, and she says, 'Chris, I'd like you to meet Roger.' And you look at her strangely because she said that without moving her lips. 'Hi, Roger what do you do for a living?' 'Actually I'm a dentist.' Have you ever tried to get through a party without opening your mouth? Drinking's fine, scotch through a straw tastes okay, and you can smoke too, just about . . . but eating? You open your mouth even a fraction and he's in there. 'My word, what an interesting mouth; when did you get the bridge done?' They're obsessed with their work. They sit opposite you on the subway waiting for you to yawn."

The spotlight was blinding him now, burning into his eyes like a sun. The party scene in his head kept playing over and over like a film rewinding and fast-forwarding. A tingling in his fingers was starting, through his hands and up his arms. There was room at the party, a locked room.

A girl in a purple leotard brought him a drink and he swallowed it quickly. He was used to the blackouts over the years, thought he had controlled them but he had never had one on stage before. Quiet murmurs were rippling through the audience, they needed another gag but his mind was a blank, except for the vivid colours of the party.

"I expect a lot of you guys out there are married? Great isn't it, marriage I mean, I used to be married, a long time ago, left her." His mind was racing. He'd never used his failed marriage for material before; it was a taboo subject for him. "She was a great lady, good cook, a terrific home-maker, sensational in bed . . . so my friends told me." The laughter rose quickly but fell even faster. The atmosphere had altered and the audience were becoming aware of it.

"Would someone dim the lights?" The spotlights faded and the houselights came on. His mind was swimming, the words were coming out but he had no control over them. He could see the audience now, see the puzzled expressions on their faces. The laughter had died away to a trickle. He could hear his voice but it seemed as if it was coming from the back of the theatre. The glass he was holding slipped from his fingers and smashed on the stage.

"He' s drunk," someone said. "High as a kite."

The microphone was getting heavier, almost too heavy to lift up to his lips. The voices from the audience were amplified, and he could hear each person clearly.

"This guy's a joke, not his act," a large redheaded woman said loudly to her companions.

Fields, swayed to the front of the stage. "Lady, when was the last time you checked a mirror? The joke'll be staring straight back at you." He was so hot, the sweat pouring down his back.

"Are you going to let him speak to me like that?" the woman demanded of a man at her table, probably her husband.

The man shrugged. "He just did."

Fields snorted into the microphone before it dropped from his grasp. "American manhood at its finest."

The man stood up, red faced, picked up a half empty champagne bottle and threw it at the stage. The bottle flew soundlessly through the air, and Fields watched it coming. It was in slow motion. Spinning above the heads of people, spilling its contents onto the tables. People were standing, wiping their clothes, but the bottle was tumbling through the air towards the stage. Fields felt everything had slowed, the room had taken on a quality of being almost stationary, and he could see the bottle slowing as it approached him.

Then it seemed to halt in mid-air, he blinked, and it smashed, broken glass and the remains of the wine falling like cruel rain onto people. The pretty blonde he had noticed earlier stood screaming, glass embedded in her low cut cleavage, blood staining the swell of her breasts.

The audience erupted, several angry faces turned to the stage, people shouted insults at Fields. "I remember my first drink," he slurred at them.

Then a bright white light exploded in his eyes. He dropped to his knees as the pain invaded his head. He felt as if a steamroller was massaging the back of his neck moving steadily forwards to his forehead. *'MORELAND.'* The word . . . name? Flashed into his head. The theatre melted away like ice, leaving him isolated on the stage, the rest only blackness. All the noise had faded, and he was left in a dark, silent void, a womblike softness in which he was trapped. The pain in his head was intense, and he cried out with the force of it as it spread through his body.

He was dimly aware of being lifted away, as purple-clad dancers milled around him, a diversionary tactic while they hauled him off the stage.

Then he collapsed into the arms of smiling unconsciousness.

Whitney settled into his sumptuous office and ran through the schedule for the day. He'd taken a Valium at midnight, on the plane, and it had given him heartburn. The cognac he'd drunk two hours later reacted with the tablet to give him a pounding headache, which returning to the isolated centre would do nothing to dispel. He let out a long sigh. The meetings had been hard work, with the first being yet another justification for the continuance of around one hundred and twenty military and scientific personnel, and more importantly for the renewal of the major funding that was required. Whitney was a failed scientist who had drifted into administration and found that he was good at it; but he also hated it. This led his bitterness down fruitless tracks until it discovered a target worthy of his frustration. At present it was the new psychic subject, Frank Moreland.

The research centre had only been in existence, unofficially, for five years, and officially did not exist at all. This made the rounds of cash collecting from the various interested departments doubly difficult, but Whitney was proud that he'd succeeded again. It wasn't easy explaining to practical minded generals that psychic phenomena could be a viable defensive strategy. 'Mind games' was one of the more polite but dismissive phrases they had used. Fortunately there were other, more covert, organisations that had access to the President's attention, and through a system of wheeling, dealing and out and out hard bargaining, Whitney had gained another eighteen months stay of execution for the centre. To get that he had mentioned on several occasions that Frank Moreland might possess some phenomenal capabilities. Now the tests would have to show whether that was true or not.

Ray Norris sat at the control panel in the lab, listening to the tracers on the EEG machine, looking up at the TV screen above his head. He made some adjustments to his computer program. The TV screen was connected to a small closed circuit camera in Frank Moreland's room, adjacent to the lab. Moreland was sleeping on a single divan bed, electrodes wired to his head to monitor his brainwaves via the electroencephalogram, and other parts of his body were wired up to a Vital Signs machine, so that every aspect of his sleep patterns could be recorded.

The tracers on the EEG jumped and Norris made a note of the data sheet on his computer. He checked the digital clock on the console. Six thirty a.m. Norris smiled, because so far Moreland's sleep patterns were uniform and predictable. Norris stretched wearily; two more hours and the night shift would be over. Two more hours and he could go back to his rooms in the staff quarters, where his wife would be waiting for him, a hot foaming bath filled and ready. Nicole would wash him, massaging his body with her supple fingers, easing away the tensions. Maybe she would slip off her robe and join him in the water, where they might make love, gently but passionately, as they tended to do quite often, being married barely three months.

Ray was twenty-nine, black, still built like the football player he had been at college. Nicole was two years younger, kept her body in fine shape with daily aerobics classes and ate only health food.

It was quiet in the lab with just the low murmur of equipment or the buzz of a printout in the background. Ray's partner on the shift, Bob Keating, came back in, delicately holding coffee and doughnuts.

"Place is like a maze."

Keating hadn't been at the centre long and still maintained a sceptical 'seen it all before' attitude that rankled the usually easy going Norris.

They ate and drank in silence before Norris said, "We have alpha and beta waking rhythms established. He's awake."

On the TV screen Moreland's body wasn't moving. "Looks like the monitors have got it wrong." Keating said, and managed to make it sound as if this wouldn't have happened in the east coast lab he used to work in.

Norris shook his head. "No, he's awake, it's just that he's sent his mind freewheeling through the centre for some exercise before he joins us."

Keating gave a 'bullshit' look but checked the computer readings before he said anything. He knew Moreland had come with some highly regarded ratings and if Norris was saying that Moreland had sent his mind roaming around, then Keating knew that was probably true.

Keating also knew, because he had sneaked a look at Moreland's dossier that the new star on the block came with a lot of excess baggage.

⁂

The sleek black limousine swung into the drive of a huge old house on the fringes of the city. Rain fell in a fine mist, clouding the windshield, making the outside of the house shapeless, almost transparent.

Imogen sat in the back of the car, flanked by the flame haired woman and the blonde. The black haired one sat opposite, next to the one Imogen feared the most. She was perhaps the most beautiful, but certainly the cruellest. Her hair was brown, verging on auburn mixed with gold, and her eyes were of the very palest violet blue. It was she who had grabbed Imogen's hand and bitten off her finger, spitting it from the window of the car.

Imogen avoided the women's baleful eyes, and cradled her mutilated hand, staring down at her feet. The hand was throbbing, the raw, jagged pain making her want to cry out, but struggled with the impulse, keeping it at bay. The car stopped and the two women next to Imogen dragged her from the back seat. She was too weak to walk so they pulled her across the gravel drive to the open door of the house.

"Where are we?" she asked but the women ignored her. Her mind struggled to make sense of the images her eyes were giving her. The house maintained a vague shape, and in her blurred state of vision she imagined it as a beast, crouched, breathing, waiting for her to enter; or perhaps a black cloud rolling towards her, ready to swallow her whole. She had the impression of rain cascading over the high gabled roof, bouncing off cold glass window-eyes, and then she was pushed through the door. The women let go of her and she fell in a heap onto the marble floor of a grand entrance hall. She closed her eyes, feeling sleep coming rapidly to her despite the white-hot fire burning in her hand. But they weren't going to let her sleep.

Savage fingers snaked into her hair and yanked her to her feet. The black haired woman held her at arms' length and slapped her across the face. Then she hit her again.

"He is waiting for you." It was the first time any of the women had spoken since they'd snatched her from the plaza. The voice was soft but guttural, accent-less, and totally expressionless. There was little overt menace in the voice, but neither was there any trace of warmth. It was a voice devoid of humanity. A form of madness burned in the woman's eyes as she tightened her grip on Imogen's hair and hauled her across the marble floor. To the right was a heavy ornate oak door its panels carved intricately. It was too dark in the house, no lights lit at all, but Imogen gained the impression of hundreds of faces staring at her from behind the door, hundreds of mouths open.

The door swung slowly open. Elsewhere she could hear muted music, a band playing, and people laughing; glasses clinking, and feet dancing, uncluttered enjoyment as a party reached full swing.

The woman pulled Imogen into the room, pushed her in the small of the back and sent her reeling to the far wall. The door shut behind them and darkness enveloped them, broken only by pale moonlight filtered in through glass panels in the ceiling.

The air in the room was foul, a fetid animal stink that made her want to retch. She stretched out her good hand and felt for the wall, following its smooth surface until she reached the corner. There she crouched, nursing her hand, feeling the uncarpeted floor beneath her, waiting.

From the far side of the room came a faint rustling, and the sound of something sharp scratching the floorboards. The air in the room was getting warmer, the smell made it almost unbearable. From across the room something moved, something large and heavy. Imogen heard the boards creaking under the strain. Then she felt hot breath on her cheek. She looked into the darkness and saw two pinpoints of blue light, blue fire. A scream rose to her throat and died there. In the black, foul-stenched room there came a roar, as if of triumph.

Then the slaughter commenced.

Robert Moreland and his wife Rebecca had headed west, away from the centre of the city, towards the fringes of Boston, where houses were large and infrequent. The road straightened, twisted, until Robert turned the Jaguar into a sweeping gravel drive with aged magnolia trees lining up either side, evenly spaced along the edge of neatly clipped lawns.

The house in front of them, as they parked the car next to dozens of others, was large, old colonial mansion style, commanding and clearly immaculately maintained. A Virginia creeper crept slyly up one side of the face of the house, a half unshaven beard partially obscuring the latticed windows.

Running to avoid the rain they reached the huge portico and rang the bell for entrance. Uniformed valets at the entrance led them into a marble floored entrance hall beyond which, through an ornately carved oak door, they could see a chandeliered ball room where seemingly hundreds of people were dancing to the music of a full orchestral band, drinking, eating, talking and generally having a good time.

"Pinch me," Rebecca whispered to her husband.

"Was that pinch or punch?" He smiled. He was thinking the same as she, what were they doing here?

Sounds of laughter and glasses clinking in celebration. The room was vast as they entered, people smiling at them as they wound their way to the bars. A piano was playing solo now, the tune *'Moonlight'*, the band having a short break. Most people were sitting, sipping their drinks, or visiting the tables laden with food.

Robert took two glasses of champagne from the tray carried by a waitress and handed one to Rebecca.

A man walked past them and caught Rebecca's arm with his sleeve. "Oh, I do beg your pardon," he said graciously. Robert thought his fat, florid face looked like a bullfrog.

Rebecca dug him in the ribs. "I know what you're thinking. Stop it." She laughed. "Where's the host? Do you see him?"

Robert shook his head. "I've only spoken to his aides on the telephone and corresponded by e-mail. I have no idea what he looks like."

Rebecca gave him a look, one of which he was fondly familiar, even though it was her, 'are you serious?' look. The truth was they had been invited to a party at the home of a potential new client whom Robert, or his assistant Daniel Parker, had never actually met. The evening was the man's suggestion, 'no business talk, let's just get to know one another in a cordial atmosphere', and Robert was pleased to accept. He was annoyed at first when Daniel and Imogen couldn't make it, but when Daniel confided the reason he wanted to be alone with her that evening Robert slapped him on the shoulder and wished him good luck.

The pianist had move into some light classics now, performing his best with some Brahms, Beethoven, and Grieg, but the overall mood in his performance was cocktail lounge rather than concert hall.

A thin gaunt woman with lilac dyed hair strolled past. "Nice party, isn't it?"

Robert and Rebecca slung back polite smiles. "Shall I get us some food?" Robert suggested.

"Don't leave me on my own, for God's sake," she pleaded. "I'll come with you."

There was a throng of people around the food tables, but there was so much food, on so many tables that they managed easily despite the crush. Robert searched the sea of faces for someone who appeared to be the host but no one was obvious in the role. They began to play 'spot the host' as they ate the delicious food.

One hot summer's night a young Robert Moreland had taken Abby Hall to the senior prom. They'd been dating all summer and he was convinced he was in love with her cornfield yellow hair and her blue lagoon eyes. He'd tried to impress her, and thought naming the tunes the band were going to play, in sequence, before they actually played them would be enough to convince her that he was the boy for her. She had been impressed at first, fascinated as he got the first two songs. He thought he was getting all the right responses from her, a kind of awe mingled with admiration, but as the evening wore on he failed to notice the subtle shift in her mood. She withdrew quietly into herself, like a hermit crab into its shell, shooting him the occasional curious look. When Tim Spalding came over to ask her to dance she was on her feet and in his arms before he'd even finished asking the question. She spent the rest of the evening with Spalding and went home with him. Robert never dated her again and the other students were quick to pass the word that Abby didn't want to be seen with a freak like Moreland. Robert was devastated, and the child in him died as he made his first adult decision. The gift, power, curse, whatever it was that he'd been born with, was something private and not a trick to be paraded for its own sake.

He was born one of triplets, his mother dying on the birthing table. Her mind, though they hardly knew it at the time, was one of immense psychic powers, allowing her at various times, depending on her state of health, and various external factors, to predict events, 'see' people miles away, move objects, and generally be sensitive to mood and surroundings. This gift she passed to each of her sons, though it had divided them since they became adults and chose to use those powers for different purposes.

Robert used his to run a successful company that dealt with recruitment and training, using his powers modestly for assessment of people and their characters. He didn't often talk about his two brothers.

Rebecca was thinking about her sister. Like Robert she was secretly pleased that Daniel was finally going to ask Imogen to marry him, they'd been dating nearly two years now. Even so Rebecca couldn't help but feel a stab of sadness that her little sister, whom she still considered her baby sister, was growing up. When they were small Imogen would always ask Rebecca's opinion without actually coming out and making it obvious, a trait she had carried over into adulthood. Often, when their parents were out for an evening, Rebecca would be left with baby sitting duties, cuddling Imogen on her lap brushing her hair, and reassuring her that she was still 'sugar and spice and all things nice'.

"What are you smiling at?" Robert touched her arm.

"Was I smiling? Just wondering how Daniel and Imogen are getting on."

At her name Robert felt an intense pain throb through the frontal lobe of his brain. He flinched.

"Are you all right?" Rebecca was instantly concerned.

Looking pale and shaken, Robert rubbed his forehead. The flash concerned him, because they were infrequent, but usually heralded trouble.

Rebecca was speaking but he couldn't really hear what she was saying. She started to walk away and he guessed she was going for help. He didn't want a fuss, but at the same time he needed a few moments to see if he could locate the source of what had sent such a powerful psychic message to him.

Zoë Mills made some adjustments to the Random Image Generator being set up for the Osis Experiment she and her colleagues were conducting later that morning with Frank Moreland. She was unaware that Frank's mind had escaped during the night, and was currently being tracked down by a frantic Norris and Keating, but had she known she wouldn't have been surprised. Moreland came with a few problems, the most inconvenient one as far as she was concerned being that he was a maverick.

Zoë was a thirty-two-year-old blonde whose looks could have provided her with a living as a fashion model or actress if she hadn't dedicated her life to science. In fact she was so dedicated even Whitney was concerned she was becoming obsessive. Her performance profiles were all A-rated for her work but gave less flattering assessments of her personal qualities. She was popular, and fairly easy going, but she had a stubborn one track mind when it came to her work. When Moreland deviated from that line she left him with no doubt that he had annoyed her.

⁂

In the computer room Norris breathed a sigh of relief when the computer readings gave a surge, revealing Moreland was whole again. He nodded to Keating who gave a sour look and bit into one of the doughnuts, dripping jelly down his chin.

"Frank?" Norris spoke into the microphone on his desk. "You *are* there?"

On the TV screen he watched as Frank's body stirred under the covers. Frank's eyes opened and he smiled. "Cold out there today."

Norris grinned. "You shouldn't have been out there at all."

Frank sat up and peeled the electrode pads from his chest. "Had to check Zoë has got things organised."

Keating spoke, a little too loudly as he was some distance from the microphone. "Zoë will have your balls if she knows you've been on walkabout again."

Standing now, and stretching his limbs Frank smiled. "She looked fine, when I visited her in the shower this morning."

Keating's mouth dropped. Norris shook his head. "He's kidding you, Bob. Aren't you, Frank – and no cracks about Nicole. Okay?"

"I need to get dressed and you two don't want to watch that. See you later."

⁂

Zoë was helping Chad Harley set up a projector in a metal box as part of the basic experiment. Chad grunted as he took the weight of the box and hoisted it onto the table. The 'mind in the box' experiment was a basic one, a variation on the stage illusionists and magicians idea of guessing the number someone was thinking of, or guess which playing card is yours.

By the time Frank entered the room the whole set-up was ready.

Whitney was already there and he hurried across to Frank, determined to make a fuss of his financial lifeline. "Frank, good night's sleep?"

Frank nodded. He thought Whitney was a pain, a necessary evil of the job, but a pain nonetheless. "Sure, very comfortable with wires sticking out of my ass."

Whitney winced. "Sticking out . . . "

"He's joking, Walt," Zoë said, and punched Frank lightly on the shoulder. Then to Frank she said, "You *are* ready? No travels this morning?"

Frank looked away but he was surprised Zoë knew about that. "Travels? Slept like a baby, Zoë. Feeling fit and well, and ready for today's little games."

Whitney made a sound between a snort and a disapproving sigh. "You wouldn't call them 'games' if you had heard the negotiations I've just had to undergo to keep this place funded. 'Games'? That was no game I can assure you." He walked off to the sanctuary of his office.

Zoë laughed. "How to win friends, Frank?"

Frank sat on the high stool that was his first position for the initial experiment. "Let's party."

Rebecca felt lost and alone, even though the party was in full swing again, now that the band had started up. She was worried about Robert, and wanted to find the host so she could get Robert to a side room, and order a paramedic if necessary. He wouldn't like it but she had seen that look on his face before, usually preceding a blackout.

Four young women were seated at a table near the entrance hall, they were talking animatedly, laughing, gossiping. Rebecca looked at them enviously; they didn't seem to have a care in the world.

The women looked across at her, curious, not staring, casually watching another party guest. Rebecca noticed their clothes, expensive and elegant, the latest designer fashion. Their hair was perfectly done, their jewellery discreet and tasteful. Then she noticed their eyes. Each of them seemed to have perfectly blue eyes. Rebecca smiled inwardly; they must have been wearing contact lenses to match each other, what a conceit.

The red headed one then stood and came over to Rebecca. "You look a little lost. Can we help?" Her voice was soft and gentle, reassuring and helpful.

"I'm Rebecca Moreland. My husband, Robert, he's not feeling too well. Do you know where our host is? I need some help."

The other women had joined them now. "Sure," the blonde one said. "We'll take you to him."

Two of them took hold of Rebecca's arms and guided her towards a door. Rebecca tried to pull away but the grip on her was tight. Their eyes were all around her, she was drowning in them. Everywhere she looked the blueness was there, like the sea and the sky merged into one. She felt her mind start to swim, feeling faint. The eyes, the blue, and then an appalling stench, like a zoo. Her head started to pound, and her movements felt muffled, jerky and uncertain.

She knew she was still inside the house, still within the entrance hall, but everything seemed so unclear. There were so many doors, and the sound of music, laughter, and glasses clinking. There was a vast room, and the women led her into it. A crystal chandelier suspended like a web from a ceiling covered in heavy bas-relief gilt work. People, countless people, sipping drinks, talking and dancing. Tables laden with food, buckets of ice. Somewhere a piano was playing 'Moonlight'. 'They've brought me back to the party,' Rebecca thought, and she turned to the women but they had gone.

The music started to get louder, stopping her thoughts, deafening her. Surely the other people didn't appreciate it this loud? She asked a couple standing next to her. The dewy blonde sniffed. "Have fun."

People were laughing and talking so loudly now that they competed with piano. "Stop!" Rebecca shouted. "Let me sleep." A face came close to hers, a fat florid face. "Eat drink and be merry," the face said, then it was gone, replaced by the face of a frog.

"You look funny," Rebecca giggled, then caught herself. This wasn't funny at all. Words came into her head but she couldn't make them reach her mouth. The music was becoming unbearable. If only she could find Robert, he'd make the music stop and the faces go away.

She pushed to the centre of the dance floor and people moved aside to let her pass. When she got there she was confused, why was she here? Swaying slightly, perspiration prickling out all over her body, eyes blinking rapidly. She looked down at herself, at her cleavage, her breasts. Her nipples stood hard and erect. She threw her arms across her chest, but everyone was laughing.

"Drunken whore," someone called out. "Just like her mother."

"No," Rebecca said softly, still swaying, shaking her head from side to side, denying the words, trying to clear her mind.

"Just like her mother, just like her mother."

A thin gaunt woman in a lilac dress with hair dyed to match came up and pinched her on the arm. "Wake up, Rebecca, you're dreaming," she said kindly.

Rebecca smiled. "Oh, am I?"

The woman forced her face to within an inch of Rebecca's, her breath fetid. "No. It's real, all of it, real!" she screamed at her.

"Please stop." Rebecca was crying, sobbing silent tears. "Please I don't want to play anymore."

The crowd of faces slowly backed away, but she felt tired, as if she wanted to sleep. Her eyelids flickered teasingly; wouldn't it be nice to lie back and fall asleep? She felt herself falling, drifting down, as light as a feather, floating, and a medley of song appeared in her mind, Sinatra, and she called for Robert.

"Rebecca? It's all right, I'm over here."

She opened her eyes and through the crowd of people she could see double doors, and they were open. The people formed into two rows facing each other, and she could see a figure standing just inside the double doors.

"Come on, Rebecca, over here."

"Party seems to be going well," a voice from the rows of people said.

"She's just a whore, like her mother."

Rebecca ran, but the more she ran the further away the figure seemed to be. She pumped her legs but it was as if she was running in deep swirling water. Faces turned to her but they weren't faces at all, just flat parchment expanses of white skin; no eyes, no mouths, no hair, nothing human.

Around her a soft sibilant chant. " . . . whore . . . whore . . . whore."

She tried to block out the voices but as she ran the faceless people reached out, long spindly fingers catching the material of her dress, scoring and tearing it. It was impossible to run any faster but the double doors seemed just as far away now. Her vision faded, then cleared, then faded again. The figure beyond the doors was walking away. It was Robert, she knew it was. Running faster, not minding who she knocked out of the way, she elbowed people to get to the doors, and she pitched herself forwards and she was through them.

It was a long passageway, with a flight of stairs at the end. The figure of the man, of Robert, was ascending the stairs. At the top was another passageway, darker, save for a single shaft of light coming from a half opened door. She went into the room.

"Robert?"

He took her in his arms and kissed her, a long lingering kiss, of people no longer strangers to one another. His tongue flicked out and hers responded, so grateful for his strength. Delving deeper into the velvet smoothness of his mouth she relished the sweetness of his comfort. She wanted to tell him she loved him and how they should never be apart again, for whatever reason, but no words came. She felt a hardness press against her and she moaned softly in her throat, returning the pressure, flattening her breasts against his firm chest. As her mind wondered how she could be so wanton, her body answered.

The kiss seemed to last forever, effortless and passionate. His hands stroked her back, caressing her skin through the thin material of the dress, and she felt his fingers reach for the clasp. The zip was pulled down, slowly and warm dry hands slipped inside and began stroking her shoulders. The dress fell to the floor and she stepped out of it as they edged towards the bed. Carefully she undid the buttons of his shirt, slid her hands onto his chest, as he removed the clip that held her hair.

His lips travelled downwards and she thrilled as they settled in the angle between her neck and her shoulders. His hands began to tease her legs, along and between them, bringing her arousal to a scream of passion. She unzipped his trousers and thrust her hand inside. He reached beneath her and drew away her flimsy clothing, touching her lightly before taking a nipple in his mouth and sucking hard.

As she raised her legs she first noticed the faint animal smell and gave a seconds thought about their surroundings. It had a familiar smell to it, and made her think of blue eyes. Then another wave of pleasure swept over her and she forgot everything else.

Their movements together were slow and lazy, as if there was all the time in the world. The earlier urgency had passed, and she was content to lay back and let his hands roam across her body, searching out sensitive places, lingering for long moments before letting her float back down again.

She gave a gasp of pain as something rough brushed over her breast. The animal smell was becoming intense, and for the first time she started to feel a flicker of unease nudging at the back of her mind. Her thoughts were blurred, but suddenly she knew something wasn't right. Why hadn't he spoken? Robert always spoke to her as they made love.

Rebecca tried to say his name but he rolled on top of her and she grunted at the weight of him. The animal musk was overpowering, sweet and corrupt. She encircled his body with her arms, but his body was covered with thick bristling hair, rough and coarse. This wasn't right; Robert's back was virtually hairless.

She opened her eyes, and at first couldn't see anything, just darkness. Then she could just make out, very faintly above her, two pinpricks of cold blue light. She was being kissed again but the tongue filled her mouth, huge and swollen as the hard lips tried to push hers into her face. His teeth sank deep into her lower lip and as blood poured into her mouth she screamed in pain and shock.

Through the coverlet of darkness in the room she could faintly make out the face of the figure on top of her. The blue eyes blinded her but even so she recognised the sneering face, although she hadn't seen him for years.

"Michael." She spoke the name of Robert's brother, and tried hard to encapsulate all the disgust she felt for him. "Is this your way of paying Robert back? By raping his wife?"

She attempted to lift herself from the bed, but his weight pinned her there, and worse he was forcing her backwards, causing her legs to open as though in invitation. Inhumanly huge it entered her, thrusting and she felt herself tear, with pain beyond expression. Her eyes closed involuntarily but before they did she saw the figure she thought to be her husband's brother, and it had more the appearance of a beast, large, covered in hair, with burning blue eyes, and additional limbs hanging loosely from its bloated body.

In her mind she saw Imogen's face. 'He's hurt me, Imogen.' 'I know.' 'Is it bad?' Imogen nodded slowly. 'Am I going to die?' 'Yes you are.' Tears welled up in Rebecca's eyes. 'They said I was a whore like mother, but she wasn't, was she?' Imogen shook her head and smiled. 'Sugar and spice just like you.'

Something huge towered over her, something ancient and evil, and hot animal breath fanned her face. Cold blue eyes bore into Rebecca's, and she became aware of four other shapes in the room.

"Is she dead yet?" the brown haired woman asked.

The beast shifted and wrenched free.

"She is now," the red headed one giggled.

⁂

Frank Moreland wasn't yet aware that something was about to go wrong. The experiments he was taking part in were routine, something he had done in one form or another since he had first arrived at the research centre about three months ago.

He wasn't yet aware that he was soon to be reunited with his two brothers, neither of whom he had seen, through choice, for more than ten years.

As soon as he realised what powers he shared with them he upped and left. About a year after that the headaches began. Often during the attacks he would get a strange floating feeling, as if he was away from his body looking at it from above. He checked into a local hospital where they scanned his brain for tumours, gave him an all clear and some pills to ease the headaches. The headaches didn't stop and the pain grew worse, until he found the only way to ease it was to allow himself to give in to the floating feeling, and let it carry him away. If he fought it the headaches continued and intensified. It wasn't long before he found he could travel with his mind, predict things, hear and see things he didn't want to see or hear, or experience at all. Then the nightmares started.

He dreamed about being in a pit, and about hearing an awful lot of screaming coming from a bamboo hut on the other side of a clearing. He dreamed a lot about the bamboo hut. Sometime the black shirted guards would pull him from the pit and drag him towards the hut, and he'd fight them, hear the screams as usual, only this time they were his own. Then he'd wake, sweating and terrified but never knowing what there was in the hut to be afraid of. The thing that frightened him the most was that every time he dreamed about it the hut came a little nearer.

It was then that he sought help. He tried an analyst but that did no good, so drink was next. Climbing inside a bottle like an alcoholic genie was a good escape, because once he'd drunk himself into a stupor he could sleep without dreaming. That treatment lasted for almost three years but before those three years were through he was out of a job, and the only way he could continue to live was to sell his house. With the money raised from that he found there were other ways to conquer his dream. He headed for New York where people minded their own business but where it was easy to find a cloak for his troubles.

That was where Chad Harley found him, at a drug rehabilitation centre in Brooklyn. The woman who ran the centre was a retired doctor called Iris Monkton, and as she weaned him off heroin she took a particular interest in the floating feeling Frank described. At one of their sessions Chad Harley was present, and Monkton told Frank it was Chad he should be speaking with.

At the research centre they began mutual experiments about the extent of Frank's abilities, and the root cause of the nightmares.

Zoë made a final adjustment to the monitors and pulled the microphone down to the level of her mouth.

"Can you hear me, Frank?"

"Loud and clear." He was in an adjacent room. His head was connected to electrodes that fed into a metal box, monitored by an EEG, and leading into the RIG. The idea was that he would *throw* his mind into the metal box and *read* the images that appeared.

"Okay, we're off." Zoë nodded to Chad, and the tracers on the EEG immediately scratched into life, indicating that Frank was already experiencing an *out of body* as an energy force had left his body.

Chad made a note on the pad in front of him. "Strain gauges show a fractional difference in pressure inside the box. The pressure rising at point two per ten seconds, with constant weight increase over the scale. An energy mass measurable in weight and pressure has entered the box."

Zoë glanced above their heads to the metal box. As always she was fascinated by her work.

"Blue tiger." Frank's voice seemingly disembodied, as if speaking through a tannoy system, and partly slurred as if in a dream, carried over the lab speakers.

A lab assistant checked the printout from the box. "Blue tiger image, right first time."

"Yellow butterfly."

"Red dog."

Each time the assistant confirmed the answers as correct.

The readings went on for three quarters of an hour. Some responses came within seconds and others needed a couple of minutes.

"Green ship."

"Blue ship, with blue people in a blue sky."

Chad touched Zoë's hand on the desk to indicate the computer screen. The EEG was showing more violent patterns.

"Nothing to worry about. " Zoë said. "As the length of time increases so Frank's mind gets tired and so the brain impulses register higher readings."

Then the strain gauges they were monitoring took a huge dip, showing a greater weight had entered the metal box.

Frank's voice came over the speakers, sounding tired. "Green man . . . no, it's not a man . . . it's, well it seems like a man but the edges keep blurring. I can't seem to get this one."

The microphone began to crackle and Frank's voice was obscured as a whistle-like amplifier feedback shrilled through the lab. Chad adjusted the controls, but Frank's voice was still obscured, this time by a sound like someone breathing.

Zoë and Chad looked at each other but neither spoke.

"We still have visual, but we've lost sound for the moment," one of the assistants reported. "Wait a minute, this can't be right."

Zoë took the readings from him. The strain gauges were showing a massive weight entering the box. Chad checked the EEG machine. "The patterns are longer, very erratic. I think we ought . . . "

A deep bass roar rang out over the microphone, the snorting of an enraged bull, the fury of a nightmare. Everyone in the lab froze, and the roar echoed into silence.

In his room Frank was shaking in a frenzy of energy, tearing at the electrodes attached to his head, blood pouring from his nostrils.

⁂

Outside in the cool night air, Robert Moreland felt slightly more comfortable. He had left the crowded ballroom as Rebecca had gone in search of help. Though he couldn't explain it to her, even after all these years, there *was* no help for him, he just needed to isolate himself so he could verify the source of the energy surge he had experienced.

In a small way everybody he had ever met exuded a small power surge, just like an increase in electrical current, at various times. At job interviews when they were lying for instance, was a typical example of how he used his knowledge every day. Because he was sensitive to it, as were his two brothers, he could tune into the variances in energy that people secreted with ease. Where he ran into trouble was when the surge was so great, the energy force so huge that it threatened to overload his ability to assimilate the information. Then he needed to be alone, to let his mind open and receive.

'Sugar and spice, just like you.'

The words were into his head before he knew it.

He was sitting on a low wall that contained an ornamental pond. A splash in the water drew his attention and a huge bullfrog had his head above the surface.

'Eat, drink and be merry.'

Suddenly the glass doors back into the house slammed shut, and the sounds of the party inside dimmed. In fact they lights had dimmed as well, and the room that just a few moments ago had been alive with music and dancing was now in virtual darkness.

A pain lanced through his eyes, stabbing at the front of his brain. He felt a sharp jolt in his left arm, and it jerked slightly before the pain subsided. He closed his eyes and his mind searched out Imogen, but he couldn't find her. Then he tried for Rebecca, but ominously he couldn't immediately locate her either. Something was there, something large, but it kept eluding him, other shapes clouding his view, distracting his thoughts.

Then pain, he could feel pain, though not his own. An animal smell all around him, and moans, but not of pain, cries of pleasure. He was getting an erection; there was the musky smell of sex, of arousal.

He tried to send his mind through the house but he met resistance. It felt familiar, but stayed at the edge of his probing, so that he was aware of an immense power but couldn't locate it.

Opening his eyes he pulled at the handles of the glass doors to the ballroom and wasn't surprised to find they opened easily. The doors opened and he crept into the house. The first thing that struck him was the musty smell, as though the house had been shut up for years, with no one living in it. Yet only ten minutes ago he had been in the house, together with dozens of other people.

There was dull light coming through grimy windows set in the ceiling, pale spotlights illuminating dust sheeted furniture, shapeless objects like sleeping ghosts. A chandelier hung from the ceiling, but it was dust covered, spider webs hanging from it.

Music, he could hear music, a piano playing 'Moonlight'.

'Hello, Robert.'

The words were in his mind before he could register an intrusion. He knew the voice but tantalisingly the recognition of it eluded him for the moment. He was still struggling to concentrate. He spun round and faced a figure in shadow from the long window to his left; a man, walking slowly forwards, out of the shadow and into the pools of light.

The man was strikingly handsome, black hair swept grandly back from a high unlined forehead, thick, possibly artificially shaped eyebrows, aquiline nose, sculpted cheekbones, lips red, full, and almost feminine. Immaculately dressed in black tuxedo, white frilled shirt, black velvet bow tie. On one wrist a heavy gold bracelet, on the fingers several rings encrusted with stones that caught the occasional shaft of moonlight. As the hand lifted to shade the eyes Robert saw them for the first time; they were blue, startlingly blue, completely at odds with the black hair and skin tones. They heightened the impression that he had been constructed from the best features of several men available to a master sculptor.

Robert knew that wasn't the case, in fact he knew just where the man had originated. He had shared the same birth. This was his brother, Michael.

The blue eyes flicked over Robert, as if sensing prey. As their eyes met Robert felt a pulse through his body, but at the same time he knew it was reciprocated as the supremely confident blue eyes registered momentary doubt as their gaze locked.

"Robert, quite a surprise."

"Not a pleasant one I can assure you." Robert had not seen Michael in almost eleven years. He had looked completely different then, but the wearing of masks to cloak his true self was nothing new.

' . . . be nice, a pleasure in fact, if you could join Mr Prince at his home . . . just an informal gathering for a few friends. Please bring Mrs Moreland.'

The words were spoken into Robert's mind in an exact duplication of the telephone call he had taken at the office when the invitation to the party had been received from his potential new client.

Michael smiled and spread the beautifully manicured hands, palms upwards. "There is no new client. Do you forgive my little deceit?"

Robert was terrified, but couldn't show it, neither as an outward display, nor as any internal emotion.

"Where is Rebecca?"

The question hung like the bond that had once joined them at birth, sibling closeness linked from the womb by their separate umbilical cords, and when severed it would rupture and wither like their relationship had done. Robert gathered his strength for the answer. Whether or not his brother gave a true answer Robert would not let the reply wound him. He would be strong and resist the challenge that he knew was coming.

Michael deliberately looked around the room, letting his gaze rest on the dust and neglect, before he murmured, "Great fuck."

The pain registered in Robert's chest rather than his brain, and that took him by surprise. He dropped to his knees and Michael moved towards him, seizing the advantage.

"She's dead, Robert. Gone to her own hell. But at least she's with that frigid sister of hers. Imogen wasn't as much fun, but then you probably tried her at some time."

'He is no longer Michael Moreland.'

Robert's head felt enlarged, and his brother seemed a long way away, as if he was looking at him through the wrong end of a telescope. His features began to distort, become hazy, like a face vaguely remembered from memory. Robert tried breathing deeply but that made his head spin, his thoughts revolving like carousel horses. His hands were sweating, his arms and legs starting to tremble. A piano began to play, notes discordant, keys cracked, hollow, echoes from fists pounding on the keyboard.

There was an explosion in his head and the noise of a party crowded in like a tidal wave, greatly amplified and distorted, pools and eddies of music and voices, waves of sound leaving ripples reverberating through his mind. He could hear the piano rising above the swell, harsh and booming, crashing out minor chords and rumbling bass lines that mad the floor vibrate.

People and faces drifted in and out of focus with the rise and fall of the tide. He saw Rebecca in the centre of the room dancing with a man who appeared to have no face, no arms, no legs, just an amorphous mass, pressed into her and gripping her. Rebecca called out for help, and the mass drifted away to be replaced by a tall thin man with a blank expanse of crumpled parchment like white sheeting where his face should have been. Rebecca's eyes were wild, her hair loose and tumbling to her shoulders. The man pulled down the top of her dress to expose her breasts, and he gripped one breast with a hand that was monstrously claw-like and squeezed, digging into the soft flesh with long thorned nails until bright beads of blood stained the creamy white skin. Rebecca was screaming with pain, but something else as well, something that made Robert want to retch.

In one corner of the room a fire had started and thick black smoke was billowing across the floor. It rolled, a living thing, absorbing everything in its path, leaving a trail of blackened wasted destruction in its wake. Robert pushed himself back against the wall as the oily cloud drew nearer. It paused in front of him like a dog sniffing a bitch, and Robert could almost taste the foul stench emanating from it, his nostrils filling with the sickening smell of burnt flesh, of decaying corpses, of death and disease. He opened his mouth to scream but the smoke cloud leapt in triumph and was upon him, rolling down his throat, setting his lungs ablaze as he tried to breathe.

Small living things were attaching themselves to him, crawling down inside his clothes, scuttling over his face, suffocating him. He closed his eyes tightly, thinking that when he opened them the smoke would be gone. He opened his eyes but the blue staring eyes were still there, mocking him.

'How does it feel to lose to the brother who sold his soul to the Devil?'

The figure of his brother, with all its artificially created features, had gone, and the reality of what Michael had become was now inside him, hiding in the black cloud within him. Robert tried to concentrate on the presence in his mind. It was there, dark and brooding, waiting to pounce, wearing Robert down. Robert concentrated fiercely, pushing the darkness away, and slowly it receded, and the dark place in his mind became lighter. Gradually it began to clear, and he exerted his will until he could feel a tearing in his head. The pain grew until he thought he would black out, and then suddenly he heard a low moan, and the echoes of a silent scream in his head.

The figure that had been the host to Michael Moreland began to shimmer in front of Robert, began to take on tangible form again as if a shadow was playing onto a screen. Robert probed forward with his strength of mind and felt shock waves. He fixed the blue eyes with his, pushing deeply, increasing the tempo until he sent a single flash of energy into the brain. The impact registered as a tightening of the skin on the flawless face.

'You don't want to see what I have become, brother.'

Robert turned his eyes away and in the doorway was Imogen. She was naked, smiling, warm and friendly and she was inviting him to join her, beckoning to him slowly and seductively.

'You want her, Robert; you always have. From the moment you first saw her. How old was she then?'

"Go to hell."

'Yours or mine, Robert? I assure you mine is much more pleasant than any you can imagine.'

Imogen was coming towards him, her breasts were slippery with oil and she caressed them as she moved, rubbing the nipples with her fingers. Her pubic mound was shaved, the darkly shadowed entrance inviting him away from the terrors.

Robert breathed deeply, gathering his strength, and probed Imogen's mind. There was nothing there, she was an illusion, but then he felt something move inside the brain. He forced a surge of power into the head and saw the features of the face change. The hair turned red, the face twisted into a faded beauty, and the woman dropped to all fours and growled. Behind her were three more figures, memories of women, all crouched ready to pounce.

Robert kept his mind active, sending out a defensive shield around his mind. He knew with numbing certainty that his life was in mortal danger, and this was the most dangerous moment. He could not allow himself any weakness, no thoughts of Rebecca, or of Imogen.

Two of the women started to squabble, the black haired one and the blonde. They threw themselves at one another like cats, claws raking through skin, teeth tearing at flesh.

'I think they need a diversion.'

Robert watched as two figures were flung on top of the women, knocking the black haired one to the ground. The four women surrounded the two; Robert clenched his fists as he recognised a bloodied and beaten Rebecca and Imogen. For a moment the two sisters cowered terrified on the floor, and then the women were upon them. The red headed one sank her teeth into Imogen's throat and hot blood pumped out, causing her to tear at the face with a frenzied lust. Rebecca's arm was torn from its socket as two of the women pulled and gnawed at it, the ripped flesh falling to the floor as the bones were shredded. The soft flesh was quickly devoured, the white bones shattered, until all that was left were pools of blood, and pieces of flesh like seaweed on a shore.

Robert turned to Michael but for a moment Michael was absorbed in his illusion. The stench of the slaughterhouse was in Robert's senses, slime dripping from the walls, yet the façade was fading, leaving the reality.

Plaster on the ceiling started to flake away, falling around them. The floor was splintering, mould coating it in places. Robert looked about him. The walls were cracked, and where the double doors had been was now a blank wall. The room was sealed.

The blue eyes blinked and Robert felt the shock waves piercing his skull. He set up a force against the intruder, pushing back with his own powers, making the other retreat. When his head had cleared a little he sent a pulse into Michael's brain, trying to hurt as much as he could. The unexpected thrust was causing confusion, and he was able to probe deeply. There were dark crawling creatures hiding in the shadows, tortured broken people crying out for mercy, and in the black corners huge inhuman shapes, writhing out of gaping holes, scrabbling towards the light.

'You won't like the new me, brother Robert.'

Frank Moreland was trapped inside the RIG box. While his body was haemorrhaging, his mind was fighting a battle against an intruder who was struggling to take him over.

A blinding light had entered the box, entered his brain. At first it had appeared as two blue lights, like car headlights bearing down on him, but then the light filled the box so that he had to shrink away from it. The light shone into every corner so that there were no shadows to hide in, nowhere to run, and for Frank Moreland that was his ultimate nightmare.

His mind pulled away from the burning light, and instinctively sought refuge back in his body. The way back was barred by a wall of flame, a barrier of fire that licked around his body, driving his mind away, keeping him from safety.

'Green man . . . no, it's not a man . . . it's, well it seems like a man but the edges keep blurring. I can't seem to get this one.'

There were flickering images in his mind's eye, white noise on a TV screen, strobe light movements with the jerkiness of dreams, puppets being roughly manipulated. The presence in the box was greedy, trying to force him out, pushing him further away from his body.

A tunnel formed in front of him and he ran to it, anywhere he could run, away from the burning fire. He ran into the tunnel and felt its welcome cool caress, and its darkness. The tunnel stretched far ahead of him, the walls wet with moisture, sticky, thick like blood.

Then he fell, and as he struggled to his feet he realised he was in a pit, with mocking ochre faces grinning down at him. There was screaming, and they were dragging him out of the pit, kicking him, prodding him with the bayonets on their rifles. The bamboo hut was getting nearer.

He broke free from them and ran; back down the tunnel, bouncing off the sides.

'I assure you my hell is much more pleasant than any you can imagine.'

He fell again, tired and uncertain, and when he got up he could see that he was somewhere different. A vast plain, in virtual darkness except for a canopy of stars hanging in the sky like a huge crystal chandelier; the plain seemed to be empty. Then he saw, in the far distance, what appeared to be a giant cloud of dust rising up from the ground, but then he realised it wasn't dust but thick black smoke that rolled like a living entity, roaring into the air as if sniffing for prey. Tiny figures on the horizon ran from the smoke cloud but it engulfed them, burning them and playing with them, before spitting them out.

Standing, he turned and ran, forcing his exhausted mind to fight back. He suddenly saw an elegant ballroom, with couples dancing, a piano playing. *'Party seems to be going well.'* It was Walt Whitney, but with the body of a frog. A woman was approaching, she was naked and her body shimmered with a coating of oil. It was Zoë. *'Sugar and spice.'*

The black cloud was forming a web around his thoughts, and he was being drawn into it. He had to resist, had to escape or he would be sentenced to an eternity of mind travel, caught in limbo above the vast plain, forever watching events unfold beneath him but powerless to intervene.

He struggled against the power of the web, pushed his mind down, forcing it back towards his body. The cloud chased him, howling like a pack of hunting dogs, filling his mind with confusion, but he stayed strong. He swam through freezing waters, and jumped over fissures in the ground.

There was a woman in a bath and she was soaping her soft dark shining skin. It was Nicole Norris, her nipples distended, black and angry, long and firm. A man entered the bathroom; Bob Keating. *'Place is like a maze.'*

Frank fought back, and directly ahead he saw the tunnel. He plunged in. The tunnel lurched as if was a snake, and bucked violently; a fairground ride of plummeting and breath stopping speed. Then the tunnel disappeared and he was over the lab, watching the familiar figures scurrying about, panic uppermost in their actions.

He was back inside the room where his body lay. As he prepared to re-enter it a face materialised in his vision. '*Well it seems like a man but the edges keep blurring.*' It was a handsome face, black hair swept grandly back from a high unlined forehead, the eyes were blue, startlingly blue. Though he hadn't seen the face for years he recognised it immediately from his childhood; it was his brother Michael.

As his mind re-entered his body he was terrifyingly aware that he wasn't alone. Michael was with him.

⁂

Zoë pulled at the microphone. "Frank, can you hear me?"

There was no answer and as Chad showed her the current readings from the monitors the print feed began to churn out page after page of paper. The lab began to vibrate; chairs fell over tables began to shake, all the computers switched off, then on again. The EEG began to billow smoke across the room, the TV screen began to flash random images. In some of the pictures Frank's body continued to twitch and jerk as if a massive electrical current was passing through him. The blood was drying on his nose but his face was contorted in pain.

"Strain gauges have snapped," Chad reported.

Zoë tried to keep professionally detached but it was impossible. All the recording equipment was acting as if a huge surge of energy was flowing through it. Telephones were ringing, lights were flashing on and off. She felt a sudden chill search her body, and goose bumps rose on her skin.

Chad watched in amazement as two of the assistants suddenly rushed from the room as their bowels and bladders opened in uncontrollable action.

Overhead sprinklers started and water rained onto their heads, falling into the machines causing tiny sparks and explosions as water and electricity mixed violently.

"We're barely getting a visual on Frank now," Zoë said. "Chad, you're going to have to go in there and check he's okay."

The TV screen suddenly cleared. It was silent in the lab as the telephones and computers stopped; even the water sprinklers had switched off.

"Thank God," Chad said. "Listen. I'll go and check on Frank, but let's make sure we can monitor him first."

They adjusted the controls, and the screen remained open but the sound was gone.

Chad left the lab and they watched on the screen as he entered Frank's room. It was like a silent movie as he looked up at the TV camera in the corner. The room was so cold that even with shirt and jeans under his white lab coat Chad began to shiver. Frank was lying completely still but the closer Chad got to him the more intense was the cold.

On the TV screen in the lab the picture began to roll over and over, images flashed brightly and then the screen went blank. "Switch to the auxiliary," Zoë said.

Chad had never known such cold before. He touched Frank's shoulder; it was hot, burning hot. Frank's hand came up in a reflex movement and gripped Chad's. Slowly Frank sat up; both his arms went around Chad's body.

"Can't get the auxiliary to work," one of the assistants said.

Keating and Norris ran into the lab. "Rasky, Johnson, Agomede, they're all dead. All of them," they said, naming all the other psychics currently housed at the centre.

Frank squeezed Chad, the heat searing into Chad's body, burning the flesh on his chest. After a few moments Frank laid back down. Chad fell to the floor, dead.

In the lab the TV screen flicked on showing Frank lying motionless on the divan, Chad on the floor.

❂

Frank was resisting with all his strength because he had always known Michael was evil. Robert would never accept that three brothers, triplets born but a few seconds part could be so different, but Frank had always understood, even as a boy.

Not that he believed this was the Michael he had grown up with, the Michael he had shared a womb with. Somehow, somewhere along the route Michael had become something different.

Frank knew he couldn't hold him forever. He was tired already, and Michael was strong. Frank needed help. He was officially catatonic, his pulses normal, though slowing, deep respiratory action but no limb movement, no eyelid flutter. He was effectively in a trance, a deep sleep without dreams, his mind caught in neutral. His mind was active though, in constant battle to contain Michael, to prevent him from escaping. But he did need help, and he could only get help by calling for it.

The dials monitoring Frank went crazy for five seconds; the EEG scratched massive signs of activity, the computers recorded brain activity, high pulse readings, heartbeat, breathing and blood pressure. For five seconds Frank was alive with hyper-activity, physically and mentally. Then he settled back down to his dormant battle.

Uptown Manhattan simmered in the late afternoon heat. Streets were crowded with shoppers hurrying to beat the rush stream of traffic that would appear when the working day ended. Coffee shops and restaurants were switching table cloths and cutlery dirtied by the lunch time trade, readying themselves for the cocktail hour, and later still the evening diners, the after show eaters.

That part of the city of New York was like an elegant lady caught unexpectedly in an embarrassing situation. She was slim, usually dignified, normally cool, but the heat that attacked her was vulgar, causing her to perspire, something not usually associated with her aloofness. She was wilting in the unaccustomed ferocity of the summer sun, the heat wave causing her attractive façade to come loose at the seams. Her inhabitants were crumpled, they were irritable and tempers that should have remained on the border's edge of reasonable boiled over into argument. Sharp suited executives would quarrel where in better mood they would negotiate; bar owners once lugubrious were surly; cops moved traffic on almost before it had parked.

The lady was hot but she remained a lady; where a lesser woman might fan her legs with her skirt, this lady kept herself above such displays. Her appearance remained as outwardly calm as ever, as full of charm as always. She never forgot she was not only a lady, but also money and power, and these scents were as seductive in the heat of the day as in the cool of the night.

Julia Lopez reached the restaurant early, which was her intention, and allowed the waiter to escort her to the corner table she'd selected and gave him her order for a vodka martini. As she sipped the drink, waiting for Lewis Darcy to arrive, she went through the ideas she had considered for the evening.

She was the executive in charge of a new product launch, a perfume that Darcy's company were manufacturing and which Julia's firm, Ryder and Stern was promoting. Julia was wining and dining Darcy this evening to help smooth the transaction. Her side of the campaign had as much to do with public relations as it did with advertising slogans. She had a bottle of the perfume in her purse but she wouldn't spray any onto her skin until later; for the moment she wore no scent, just the smell of the herbal soap she had used in the shower.

The waiter hovered with the menu but she waved him away If she had summed up Darcy correctly he'd prefer to choose the meal himself, select the wine, lead the way as some men needed to do. Julia would play along until it suited her to take the upper hand. Just then Darcy entered the restaurant and he was brought across to the table, where Julia and he said the meaningless greetings that people did in situations like these.

"You found the place easily?" Julia asked him, and ordered another drink.

"I'll have a Glenfiddich, neat please." Darcy said. "Sure, no problem." He looked around at the other tables; a little after nine the restaurant was full. "Nice place. Come here a lot?"

Julia shook her head. Her hair was black; it wasn't brown, dark brown or any such variant, it was pure night black, and natural, no colourings. Her eyes provided the stars, lightly speckled brown dancing with warmth. Her skin was smooth, faintly enhanced with a minimum of cosmetics. Her body under her simple white dress was stunning. Darcy hardly heard a word of her answer.

"Would you like to order for us, Lewis?" Julia could see from his face that the trouble she had taken to look good had been worth it.

He motioned for the waiter and began to peruse the menu. Julia knew he was pleased she had asked him to choose the meal; it played to his masculine instincts and he was flattered. When their drinks arrived he raised his glass in a salute. "Here's to a successful evening."

Julia paused before she sipped her drink. "I'm sure we'll have a wonderful time, Lewis."

"So what do you think of the campaign?"

Julia laughed softly. "Shouldn't *I* be asking *you* that?"

"I guess so, but I'd like your opinion."

Julia pretended to consider a reply for a moment, giving herself time to think. She guessed he would prefer an honest opinion, but at the same time he was a hard-headed businessman and would already have considered most of the angles. "I think it's a good product . . . "

"You do?"

"Yes, I do. It's got an originality about it that I like; the name's good, the packaging is good." She laughed. "And the advertising is terrific."

Darcy laughed with her and Julia hoped she had chosen the right level of pitch. The food arrived for the first course and they began to eat. Darcy tasted the wine and nodded his approval. He must have been fifty or so, but the steel grey threading through his hair was distinguished looking. The lines in his face were full of character not age, and his clothes were immaculate.

When the first course was cleared away three waiters brought the main dishes. Julia was having British beef, and as she pressed her fork into the meat red blood oozed onto the plate.

"So, what do you do with yourself on your nights off, Julia?"

He was beginning to flirt with her as she had predicted he would. She forked a mouthful of meat from the plate and allowed it to hover tantalisingly in front of her lips. "I like to enjoy myself, like now . . . I enjoy my work." She closed her lips around the fork.

Darcy drank some wine and Julia watched him carefully. She had to play the game very skilfully, keep him hooked, let him think she was available without letting him land her.

"Do you have a regular boyfriend?"

Julia smiled. "I'm twenty nine next birthday, Lewis, boys hold little interest any more; I prefer a man to take me out . . . tell me . . . are you attached?"

A slight hesitation, and then. "Yes, yes I am."

"Are you faithful to her?"

He looked down at his plate. "I . . . I am."

Julia ran her tongue over her lips, tasting the blood there. "You're an attractive man, Lewis, how are you enjoying your meal?"

"Fine, just fine, how's your beef?"

Julia placed another piece of meat in her mouth, and as she couldn't immediately speak she placed her hand over his on top of the table. He didn't try to pull away and when her mouth was clear she took her hand away.

"It's delicious, your choice was perfect." She placed her hand back onto the table top near to Darcy's but his hand drew back. Julia smiled at him, and sipped her wine. It didn't come naturally to her to play the tease, it wasn't a part of the job that she enjoyed, but it *was* a part of the job. Darcy was a little nervous of her now and she liked that. Julia thought he would have imagined himself seducing her and now he wasn't so sure, and she began to calculate ways to say goodnight without letting him feel rebuffed.

"What have you chosen for dessert?"

The waiter brought along a huge bowl of fresh raspberries and Julia and Darcy laughed together. "I guess there's the answer."

"Here, try one." Darcy spooned a single raspberry and offered it to Julia. She lightly held his hand as she took the ripe succulent fruit into her mouth.

"I love the taste on my tongue." Next moment she was choking as the fruit was swallowed awkwardly.

Darcy stood to help her but she fumbled in her purse for a handkerchief to dab at her eyes. As she pulled out the handkerchief two photographs fluttered to the floor. "I feel such a fool." She didn't notice the photographs.

Darcy bent down to retrieve them. "Think nothing of it. So long as you're okay."

She drank some water. "I'm fine now. What have you got there?"

Darcy handed the photographs to her; they were of a boy aged about eight or nine. "Nice boy."

Julia took the photographs and held them for a moment. She didn't like anyone to see them but there was no way out now, and in any case the stupid choking had destroyed the foolishly constructed atmosphere of flirtation. "He's my son."

"That's great, he has your colouring. I didn't realise you were married."

"I'm not."

"None of my business. " He fished around in his jacket pocket. "Here, take a look at these."

His wife and three children were posed in a series of shots that spelt warmth, security and home comforts. She handed them back to him and noticed that he was laughing. She began to smile herself not knowing why. What had begun as a small chuckle was turning into uncontrollable laughter.

People at nearby tables were turning, amused at the two of them.

"Lewis . . . stop it . . . what is it?"

Darcy made a visible effort to control himself. "It's . . . I just didn't see the evening turning out like this." He took a long swallow of wine. "Sharing family snapshots. I thought I was going to have to spend the rest of the evening getting out of seducing you . . . oh, don't get me wrong, Julia . . . you're gorgeous, and I'd have enjoyed it, except . . . well, I *am* faithful to my wife."

Julia laughed out loud, throwing her head back, her hair shimmering in the subdued lighting. "I don't believe it."

"I've upset you?"

"Not at all. I thought the same as you. I wanted to keep you sweet so the campaign would go well . . . but I was trying to figure out how to let you down graciously when you came on strong later this evening."

As Darcy paid the check Julia hailed a cab. An evening she had been dreading had turned out fine; she had been herself for a moment and he had liked her that way far better than the role she had assumed for him.

When they pulled up outside her brownstone overlooking Central Park Julia realised she was a little jealous of Darcy and his happy home life. He was the sort of man she always hoped she would meet for herself. He kissed her cheek and the cab was gone.

Julia looked up at the apartment building and saw there was a light on in her apartment. Des Hooper would be awake and waiting for her, but she couldn't face another argument; she was too tired and too hot. If she waited maybe he would fall asleep; it would only postpone his griping until the morning but that would have to do for now. She sat on the front step and fanned her face with her fingers.

⁂

The three muggers were like sharks in a pool; they couldn't see the woman but they felt the ripples of her presence. They were still but when they moved it was in slow circles through the shadowed waters. They were still but they could feel her nearby and were aware of even her slightest movement. They moved by instinct nearer to her, and were still again, sheltered in the trees and bushes of the park, their natural habitat.

Julia sat quietly in the warm darkness, conscious of how ridiculous her actions were. She was well aware things weren't working out with Des; it had been a mistake to ask him to share her apartment.

The three sharks circled their prey and revealed themselves. Julia saw movement to the side of her and froze. A skinny youth dressed in denim moved away from the cover of bushes and stood motionless. Ahead of her a bulky figure appeared from the shadows, carrying a knife. Julia stood and noticed the third one, to the right and slightly behind her, tapping a stick against his leg with a soulful rhythm.

"Give us the money," one of the figures slurred.

"Let's take her."

"Let's see her."

Julia was silent, her eyes starting to blur. For a second she felt as if she was going to pass out and then she felt as if she was sleep walking. She felt apart from her body, knowing from experience what was happening to her but lacking full control over it.

The tall shark wrapped himself around her body and pinned her arms. The skinny underfed one pulled at her purse but couldn't prise it loose. The bulky one grabbed the front of her dress and squeezed cruelly.

Julia felt no pain, nor any fear. Her body went rigid and she felt a pulse beating in her brain.

The bulky shark lifted in the air and flew backwards, propelled by an unseen force, thrown through the air and landing heavily against a fire hydrant, where he shouted out in pain as he felt his leg crack.

The tall one cried out in sudden alarm as Julia's body grew red hot beneath his hands, and the skin on his fingers blistered. He jerked his arms away and held his hands to his body to try to stem the spasm of burning.

The third shark drew away into the shadows, but Julia turned to look at him. Her eyes held his and he felt his legs buckle beneath him, as he fell to the ground. He tried to stand but he had no strength left in his body. He lay beached and helpless.

Julia turned into the entrance hall of the brownstone. The moment had gone and she was back to normal, although that wasn't how she felt. She had suffered these attacks of uncontrollable energy for as long as she could remember and she was tired.

It was well past midnight and thankfully Des was asleep when she went into the apartment. She undressed and went to sleep in the spare.

In the morning she told him it was because she didn't want to disturb him but they both knew the real reason. She told him she needed a few days break, go and see her son, her parents. Maybe it would be for the best if he were gone when she got back. He handed over his key like a naughty child scolded at school.

The drive up to Albany took almost two hours. The regular payment she sent each month to her parents represented a quarter of her salary but it didn't free her from the guilt she felt for leaving her son with her parents.

Her parents had taken the news of her pregnancy well enough, even when she refused to name the father, and had supported her while she finished college and established her career. It had been their idea to look after Matt while Julia worked, and the arrangement suited them all, with the schools, the friends Matt was making, and the quality of life he was enjoying far better than he would have had in the city. It took a huge toll though in Julia's emotions.

Her parent's house was set back from the road on its own piece of land, shielded by trees from the nearest neighbours.

As usual her mother was in the kitchen making something for the lunch, while Matt and her father played in the woods or fields that surrounded them.

The weekly visits ran a similar course each time, with her mother anxious to ensure she was looking after herself correctly and her father always prepared to remind her of the sacrifices he was making on her behalf.

Matt and she were just glad to spend some time together. They caught up on one another's news, read, played and generally enjoyed being together.

When the day was over, and Matt was long in bed, the evening meal ate, and her father smoking a cigar on the porch, Julia helped her mother with the dishes. It was when she dropped a plate, the motion of it falling to the floor seemingly caught in freeze frame action that she knew something was wrong. After the attack in the park she wouldn't have expected another one so soon. Making the excuse of being tired she went to her room, largely unchanged since she had lived in the house.

Outside her window she could hear an owl as it swooped low over the fields. The aroma of her father's cigar wafted on the warm night air. The episode with the muggers flashed into her mind. Her head began to spin. In the next room she could hear Matt's slow and even breathing. Bright lights began to dance in front of her eyes. She closed her eyes but the lights were still there. Her mother was climbing the stairs, and Julia knew she would have a glass of milk on a tray. The milk was parchment white, blank like skin. *Don't drink the milk, whore just like my mother.* Pain flashed through her head and her body sat upright on the bed.

There was bright light, and burning at the mouth of a tunnel. A man was running and then he fell. Before she knew what she was doing she had pulled her case out, packed what little she had taken out and was saying her goodbyes.

⁂

Robert Moreland was already aware he had never really known his brother. Even as a boy Michael had always been different from the others. Where they would be frightened of the dark Michael seemed to prefer it; when the others crouched down into the sofa while watching old horror films, Michael would be laughing and calling it 'unreal'. Robert could clearly remember Michael having a kind of quest to find what he called the 'true horror in life'. When he learned about his psychic powers he was overjoyed, until he realised both his brothers shared them as well. Then he was mortified and swore he would do everything he could to make his powers stronger, better, different.

A fierce flame of light seared at Roberts's thoughts and he recoiled, bringing his mind away from Michael's dark mind.

The mask started to slip away; the civilised veneer with which the beast had cloaked itself cracked and fell, leaving the true horror, the true nature of the evil that lay below the surface; that had always lain beneath Michael's surface.

The layers peeled away like petals from a dying rose and the handsome man that had been created disappeared, as what Michael Moreland had become started to emerge, blinking into the gloom. Skin split, bones liquefied, as something dreadful showed its true face.

Robert moved against one wall, as far away as he could get, as the windows broke in a shower of splinters and the sky outside, unnaturally black, starless and storm-laden, closed in. Clouds across the sky caused shadows to dance in the room, where once had been people, and the shadows seemed to cry out in torment, the volume rising until Robert had to cover his ears to be able even to think. He imagined he could hear Rebecca's voice above the rest but he knew it was an illusion.

In front of him now, amorphous on the ground, was a huge shapeless mass that swayed like a black cloud, rolling and unfurling as if a shadow of someone's nightmare. All around was the stench of decay, a rotting flesh, and Robert gagged when he saw, caught up in the mass of the creature's body, corpses, some merely white bone, others with tattered flesh still hanging from the skeletons, and some, the worst sight of all, some still alive but caught and helpless. There were living things within the mass, writhing, feeding from the dead and the dying, tearing the rotted flesh from the bones.

In the corner of the room four shapes moved stealthily towards Robert; the women clothed now in torn rags, skin hanging in folds from their emaciated bodies, tongues lolling over cracked lips, as though they had escaped from the mass. The one with red hair sprang at Robert, catching his chest with her claws, but he twisted to one side as she jumped. As he felt the skin of his chest tear he swung his fist down on her head, knocking her away from him. She fell awkwardly to the floor, and before she could move Robert ran over to her, gripped her neck between his hands, wrenched savagely sideways and heard the loud crack as her neck broke.

The other three women howled, dropped to all fours and rushed at Robert. As they ran past the massive creature a tentacle whipped out and took the brown haired one. She whimpered as she was lowered into the heart of the beast. There was a fierce blaze of heat, and her body crackled as the fire took hold.

The remaining two women were picked up as if feathers; the head of one was bitten off with a crunch and the discarded body dropped into the seething mass. Robert was weakened by the constant need to keep his defences alert. With the beast distracted with the women, he edged along the wall, trying to get to the broken window. Suddenly a claw-like tentacle shot out and knocked him to the floor. He struggled to his feet, keeping his mind alert, but the room appeared to be empty. There were restless shadows all around, but he couldn't sense Michael, or what he had become.

The room was silent except for his laboured breathing. He let his mind relax, dropped his defences, and opened his senses, probing for a reaction. There was resistance immediately; the force was still in the room, and he covered his mind again, sending out waves of attack. The answer was instant and ferocious; Robert was lifted bodily from the ground and flung like a rag doll against the far wall, the breath knocked out of him. Before he could move he was lifted again and thrown against the floor, where he slumped in a heap. A huge arm whistled out of the darkness and smashed into his nose.

Despite the pain he threw out wave after wave of energy, feeling the wounds opening, and the pain he was inflicting. There were voices in his head, or were they in the room? *'Eat drink and be merry.' 'Party seems to be going well.'*

A bride stood in the centre of the room, dressed in flowing white, a thin veil covering her face. Pure white hands lifted the veil and he stared into the face of Imogen as she might have been on her wedding day. Then the dress began to crumble, the material dissolving, as Imogen's features changed; maggots crawled from her eye sockets, worms wriggled from her mouth, and blood seeped from the pores of her skin as she sagged to the floor and sank into a pool of thick liquid.

Robert felt the pressure squeezing his brain, battering his defences. The beast was materialising in the room, the huge black cloud filling half the room, expanding, rolling towards Robert, ready to swallow him.

The pain in Robert's head was too intense now, the agony of his body too deep to ignore. He needed to sleep. He felt the tentacles lick over him, slimy and possessive. He imagined he heard the cruel chuckle that Michael always gave when, as a boy, he would play a cruel trick on Robert and Frank.

Then everything was bathed in a brilliant white light. The creature, its body filling the room, seemed suddenly to shrink away from the light. Robert sent one last weakened probe into its mind and felt momentarily not one entity but two. Two powers were locked in a struggle that lasted mere moments before there was an implosion, the walls of the room seemed to crumble and Robert collapsed.

⁂

When he woke he had the taste of dust in his mouth. He coughed, a harsh rasping cough that jerked through his injured body bringing a scream of protest from his limbs. He lay face down on the floor, breathing deeply, trying to ascertain how badly hurt he was. His eyes were puffy and swollen, there was a crust of dried blood under his nose, and his ribs were aching. The skin on his chest and side was torn, but the blood had already dried.

He pulled himself to a seated position, his head throbbing, uncertain where he was. When he remembered he shrank into himself, defensive; but there was nothing here. He probed gently through the house, but the rooms were as empty as shells left stranded on a beach. His thoughts bounced back from darkened rooms and passages, like strangers avoiding each other's glances.

The house was a tomb, and he knew Rebecca was dead. With a low groan he sank to his knees, hugging himself with the physical pain of his grief. Hot tears rolled down his cheeks, as the realisation of his loss was uncontrollable. He rocked back and forth, calling her name.

Slowly he forced the pain to subside, leaving him alone and numb. There was nothing for him here. The Jaguar was outside, parked neatly on an empty drive.

⊙

Thunderheads were gathered across Boston, purple black edifices rimmed with silver, hanging threateningly above the masts of the yachts in the harbour, touching the tips of the trees on Boston Common with dark menace.

A dog whined low in its throat and slunk along on its haunches, belly-down on the sidewalk, chasing shadows in which to conceal itself, shying away from the lights. Its ears were pricked in fearful apprehension; something was hidden in the storm, and it frightened the animal's instincts, making it want to hide until whatever it was had gone. A car door slammed and the dog began to whimper, darting down an alley for comfort, crouching there, panting softly, eyes watchful.

⁂

The apartment in Hanover Street was cold and empty, flat and dead without Imogen's presence. Daniel moved from room to room restlessly, feeling like a stranger in his own home. He couldn't accept the police advice and, 'go home and wait by the 'phone.' He slammed his fist against a doorframe; he had to get out and do something. The anger and fear were welling up inside again, but the overwhelming emotion was of frustration. Frustration that he had failed to protect her; frustration that he had no idea where she was, or what was happening . . . a sob broke from his mouth and he clamped his hand to his lips to try to stem it but the tide was rising. He sat on their bed, stroked her pillow, and sobbed into his hands. He had never known such hurt, such terror before and he was frightened he couldn't cope.

They had argued at the hospital when he had announced he was discharging himself, but there was little they could do to prevent him. The nurse arrived to give him another injection and found him searching for his clothes. The doctor was called and added his protests but Daniel was adamant; he signed the waivers and disclaimers and got a cab home.

Only it didn't feel like home any more. He showered quickly and changed his torn and bloodied clothes. The black and silver Harley Davidson stood on its rest, waiting for him like an old and dependable friend. He started the engine, eased the bike from its stand, and drove out into the rain swept night.

⁂

Robert stared broodingly out at the rampant storm. The air was thick, hot and humid. He breathed deeply through his nose, sniffing the air, detecting the faint whiff of ozone.

As a fork of lightning ripped through the sullen sky his fingers clenched on the windowsill, knuckles whitening under the steady and intense pressure he was immersed in. He wanted to scream, to voice his pain, his grief; he wanted to see Rebecca again; he wanted to kill Michael; he wanted to hurt someone so that he might feel better. Anger rose like bile and as the thunder exploded above him he slammed the window shut.

A small walnut table stood in a corner of his study, and he walked to it, and poured a large Scotch from a crystal decanter. The hand that held the matching crystal glass shook so much the drink slopped over the side, bouncing from his shoe to stain the patterned Persian rug. He was still in shock, he knew that, but he had to take action. Somewhere, what was once his brother was waiting for him.

He gripped his wrist to steady it, poured some more whisky, and brought the glass up to his lips with both hands. The scotch burned his throat but he gulped it down in one long swallow. The drink focussed his mind; he didn't want a distracted mind for the work ahead of him.

Thunder growled and found an echo in the dog's throat. The sound gave way to another, a deep rhythmic roaring, and the dog looked around with frightened eyes, terrified by the single white eye glaring in the distance. As it closed in the roar got louder and the white eye blazed fiercely. The hackles rose on the dog's back and it broke from the cover of the alley, ran across the street, into the path of the oncoming Harley Davidson.

The bike's headlights speared the dog in the centre of the road, before Daniel swerved, leaned on the horn and pulled the machine out of its skid. The dog howled and raced away seeking cover in the lee of a storm drain. Daniel swore at it, and rode off, riding as fast as before, not really caring if he made it to Robert's house or not.

When he got there all the lights in the house were off, but the car was there. Using his own key to let himself in, he checked the downstairs rooms but they were all empty. He began to get a nervous feeling. Were they at the police station? Or at the morgue, identifying Imogen's body?

Robert was in the study. Both men looked at each other, appraising the physical injuries they both displayed. Awkwardly, as if acknowledging that it was others they would rather embrace, they hugged.

Daniel realised Robert had more knowledge than he did, knew more than he did about what had happened. Quietly and efficiently Robert told Daniel about Imogen, about Rebecca, and as much as he could explain about Michael.

⁂

When Robert had finished speaking they held each other's eyes in hostile silence. Daniel found he was shaking.

"What do we do now?" he asked.

Robert poured another drink, and without asking whether he wanted one, handed one to Daniel. "There's one thing I haven't told you, because I'm not sure about it myself."

Daniel drained his glass, realising they were both drinking far too much. "What else can there be to tell?"

Robert hesitated, not sure if the other presence he had felt in the house, for a split second, had been what he thought. "I haven't seen Michael for years, ten or more. I always knew he would use his powers badly; but I haven't seen my other brother, Frank, for about the same length of time."

"You had a 'falling out', you've told me before."

"Sure, Michael disappeared off to Europe, and I never heard from him. Frank went off the rails, drink, drugs, you name it; all in an attempt to escape the power he didn't want. When I thought Michael was going to kill me, in the house, when I was completely drained, another force entered the room, and if I'm right that was Frank."

"Would his power be strong enough to know you were in trouble?"

Robert looked out of the window, at the departing storm. "If I'm right, I think Frank is holding Michael, by the force of his will. The trouble is Frank isn't as strong as Michael, especially after the life he's led; it's just a matter of time before Michael, or whatever he is now, breaks free."

"What happens then?"

Robert shrugged. "I have no idea, but I think I'm his prime target. Rebecca and Imogen were pawns in his game."

Daniel helped himself to another scotch. Robert accepted his glass without acknowledgement. "So," Daniel said. "We need to find Frank."

Robert pulled a huge tongue of paper from the computer printer. "I think we already have, or rather he's found us." He gave the pile of paper to Daniel.

"What's this?"

"Look at it; it was hanging out of the printer when I got back, the computer was switched off, so God knows how it printed it."

Most of the paper was blank, but at random intervals were letters, partly formed into words. When words were decipherable they were repeated, over and over, until the letters merged into themselves. The words seemed to be 'Michael', 'Frank', 'Robert', and 'help'.

Daniel shook his head in amazement. "All we need now is an address."

Robert gave a tight smile. "Look at the very bottom, where there seems to be just a jumble of letters."

Daniel looked, walked to the lamp and held the paper close. Amongst hundreds of repeated letters, and numbers, coalesced as though someone was holding down several keys at once on a computer keyboard, was an address in Kansas.

⁂

Whitney stood in the room they had turned into a makeshift morgue; where five bodies, covered by sheets, were lying on trestle tables. In the corner a portable refrigeration unit throbbed noisily, bringing the temperature down icily. Whitney wasn't dressed for the cold and he shivered in his light cotton shirt and summer trousers. He rubbed his palms together quickly, letting friction warm them, then approached the first table.

The centre had limited medical facilities, and certainly no qualified pathologist, so the post mortems would have to wait. Unreasonably, he conceded, he blamed Frank Moreland for the deaths of the four psychics, and Chad Harley. He hated himself for it, but Whitney was already thinking about scapegoats and damage limitation, when the questions were asked, as they would be, about what had happened and who was to blame.

He lifted the corner of one of the sheets on one of the tables. There were no identification tags, so he didn't know who was under it, but he could guess by the size of the body that it was male. A terrible odour assailed his nostrils and he gagged; the smell of charred meat and the stench of death. He felt his stomach lurch and he let the sheet drop without having looked at the body. To his credit his guilt made him look, and he fought down a wave of nausea that was making his head spin, and yanked the sheet aside. He looked own only briefly but that was enough. Vomit rushed up from his stomach and into his mouth and he barely had time to turn away from the burned body before it burst through his lips in a spray, adding its own stench to the one pervading the room.

He staggered from the room, and down the corridor. His throat hurt from retching, and his legs trembled from the shock of what he'd seen under the sheet. He found himself outside another door, and he turned the handle and went in. He found himself in the centre's chapel; a much larger room than the makeshift morgue but somehow just as oppressive. The thought entered his head that he had been intending to come here all along and the visit to the morgue was merely a detour. Whitney wasn't religious; a childhood being dragged along to evangelical meetings by a fanatical father had exorcised any spiritual leanings he might have had or developed. The chapel wasn't elaborate, and Whitney knew from the complaints of Reverend Flint, the priest from Shawville who travelled in once a week to give blessings that it wasn't well attended.

Whitney walked to the front row of chairs and sat facing the altar, nervously glancing behind him to ensure he had closed the door. He didn't want anyone to find him in here, believing it would be seen as a mark of weakness. He didn't feel weak, but he was confused, and scared. For all his protestations of atheism he could clearly recall words regularly used by the travelling evangelists, 'And the sinner shall be punished by the fires of Hell for all eternity.'

When the full extent of the tragedy that had struck them was realised it had awoken fears that had lain dormant ever since he had taken responsibility for this project. The fear that they were tampering with the unknown, perhaps the unknowable, and by interfering with such forces they might be altering the very laws of nature. He couldn't dislodge from his thoughts the idea that had confronted him as soon as he had learned the extent of what had happened; they had affronted God. By experimenting with the mind, and all the unknown powers that it contained, had they tried to play god themselves? Had they invoked some kind of judgement upon themselves?

The logical side of his brain denied this possibility; but in the chapel, in the quiet, as he sat alone, he clasped his hands together, prayed to a God he wasn't even sure he believed in, and asked for forgiveness.

⁂

Zoë arrived to a lab of laughter. Chris Fields was at the centre of a group of white coats and hilarity. " . . . And the mule says to the zebra, 'That might be a fancy pair of pyjamas but are you sure that's where to stick the carrot?' " The group roared with laughter, although to Zoë it sounded false. Fields looked around at the faces; this was what he fed on, the adoration from the audience.

To say the least there had been some explaining to do when Fields, closely followed by Julia Lopez, arrived at the gates, in separate cabs, and asked to be admitted. Fields' celebrity status helped them gain access, but both had to undergo extensive vetting before they were permitted to leave the interrogation room they were initially confined to. Now they had been allocated a bungalow each amongst the staff section, and had been asked to attend a meeting where the next step could be decided.

Frank Moreland was still lying comatose, with minimal bodily responses, although Fields and Julia both claimed to have been 'called' here by him. Both had discovered they could talk, or at least communicate in a rudimentary fashion, through their minds.

Whitney came in just as Zoë was recapping what the position was. She nodded to Whitney and waited to see if he wanted to take over from her, but he seemed distracted, so she continued.

"What we need to know, so far as I'm concerned, is why Frank Moreland is in a catatonic state, and what we can do about it."

Fields, was lighting up his third cigarette, ignoring the annoyed stares and muttering around him. "I'd like to know why I'm here."

Whitney had taken an instant dislike to Fields, and was unconcerned that it seemed to be mutual. "You came here of your own free will; presumably you can leave any time you want."

Julia wanted to avoid a confrontation; because she was frightened by what she had found when she arrived. Dead people were not what she was expecting. "Mr Fields, and I can leave, with your permission, of course, but that's missing the point – what brought us here in the first place?" She looked harshly at Fields, "And don't say two cabs."

"Lady, you've seen my act."

Zoë smiled. "Actually I have, in L.A. a couple of years ago. You were good."

Fields blew a circle of smoke into the air. "Better now."

Whitney clapped his hands. "When we've finished with the banter, may I remind everyone that we have five deaths, and one man in a coma? It's answers we need, serious ones, not smart ones."

Before anyone got a chance for any kind of answer a guard knocked on the door and opened it. "There're two more at the gate, asking to be let in."

Whitney and Zoë looked at one another.

"One of them says his name is Moreland," the guard said.

When Robert and Daniel were finally admitted they were put into a holding room while various calls were made to verify identities. The police in Boston were able to confirm both men seemed to be who they said they were, but also to confirm that the girlfriend of one had been reported as missing, and the wife of the other, both women sisters, was not at home.

"Well," Whitney said, blowing his cheeks out. "It seems the police would like to have a few words with both of you when they catch up with you."

Robert was so focussed that he dismissed the threat of police questioning with a wave of his hand. If he didn't stay focussed the pain of losing Rebecca would overwhelm him. His emotions were barely held in check, his every thought involved her; his every feeling was raw and tender. Only the focus of finding Michael and dealing with him was holding him together.

Zoë ran through what stage they had reached, and wanted to know if Robert knew why Fields and Julia were here.

Daniel couldn't help notice how strained Zoë seemed. He had no way of knowing how she normally behaved but clearly she was currently under a great stress and was battling to control it. He was numb from the shock of Imogen's death, feeling as if he had been awake for a week and had lost all ability to think, or feel. He had read that it was quite a common phenomena after a funeral for the grieving widow or widower to feel incredibly aroused and even on several accounts for them to have sex with someone, usually a friend or relative, on the day of the funeral itself. He looked at Zoë and couldn't prevent himself thinking of her body, the way she pronounced certain words, and the way her hair fell across her shoulders.

"I'm here because Frank is my brother, and I think . . . let's just say, I think I know what has attacked him." Robert was saying.

"And what had attacked him, attacked the others?" Whitney asked.

Robert ignored the question as best as he could. There was not an answer he could give that would be understood or accepted. "If Frank has sent out a message, telepathically I mean, to Fields and Lopez, as well as to me, then he must believe it needs our combined powers to combat whatever it is he's trapped."

"Trapped?" Zoë hadn't realised that was what they were discussing.

"You told me about the experiment, the responses you were getting. I think something attacked Frank, and the others . . . " He looked at Whitney. "And by sheer force of will Frank was able to contain it, within his mind. But the stamina needed to do that has left him . . . well, you know what condition he's in. He can't hold out indefinitely which is why he's called for reinforcements."

⁂

Robert had been allowed to see Frank alone. The others were relaxing somewhere. After a series of tests on all of them Robert was worried; Julia had been openly relieved that what she had endured for years could finally be given a label. She was though vulnerable at present; unable to focus her power easily, though when she did the results were strong. Fields on the other hand was like a tornado, his powers wild and random, never allowing any consistency to develop. His results were actually better than Robert's on an individual level but they were too variable for Robert to be confident about them.

Frank was weakening by the hour. Still catatonic the charts showed slow but steady decline in all his bodily functions. Robert placed his hand over his brothers; it was cool, cold almost, the pulse slowed to nearly zero.

Wait, Frank tries to move his hand . . . Robert's fingers are taken in a weak grasp . . . they lay within Frank's palm . . . Frank squeezes Robert's hand.

Like a lightning bolt through his brain Robert feels Frank's chaotic thoughts trying to contact him. He probes Frank's mind.

There are only remnants of what once was there. Confusion and darkness hide merely the essence of the man that he used to know. What dominated was the evil that had attacked him, and Robert was scared to approach it.

'I am hungry, Robert.'

Robert extracted himself from Frank's mind. The body remained still but all of a sudden Frank's eyes opened; bright shining blue. Robert pushed himself away from the table, but the room had changed.

The ceiling was damp, covered in mould, breaking off in places, and falling to the floor. Green slime dripped from the walls, running in rivulets like mutated rain on a windowpane. The carpet had rotted, in places bare wooden boards showed, pitted and scarred with infestation. What carpet remained was wet, soaked through with a foul green liquid, the stench of which was overpowering. It was the smell of dank, secret places, of hidden tombs, of desecrated mausoleums; the odour of corrupt corpses, putrescent flesh torn from rank, stinking graves. Frank's divan had decomposed, fallen like a fetid creature racked with a most terrible disease. Maggots crawled over the chairs; spiders spun their webs in dark corners of the room, hooking tiny insects on unseen gossamer threads. The floor was covered with worms;

sightless they raised their wriggling bodies into the air as if sniffing for scent, then crawled over themselves in a seething mass; more flopped from the corners of tables, into the waiting sea below.

The door had shut silently behind him and Robert realised he was trapped. The room was closing in on him, a coffin forming around him. Insects dropped onto his shoulders, and as he brushed them away so worms crawled over his shoes, and as he kicked out at them, so a swarm of flies buzzed around his head. He concentrated his mind, overcoming his tiredness and his despair. He sent his mind spinning around the room, touching all the repulsive manifestations, wiping them away, sweeping the room clean.

There was silence, as the room fell back to normal. The carpets were clean, the divan was neat, and the walls white, and Frank lay motionless. The room began to vibrate.

Glass on the TV monitor cracked; equipment on the walls began to shift, slowly at first, then faster, until much of it fell to the floor. The covers over Frank were ripped off, and hurled in tatters about the room. There was fierce wind in the room, knocking over the chairs, chasing paper through the air, tossing wires and pieces of equipment around as if by a crazed juggler. Shadows stirred and shifted, and Robert thought he could see creatures of the night crawling in frightful pleasure towards him. As the wind grew fiercer, his clothes whipped around like lunatics feeling from the moon, and he was forced back against the door; his back felt the hard wood press into him and he felt the comforting solid feel of the smooth surface. Something grabbed hold of his jacket. He turned his head around; the handle of the door had transformed into a claw-like growth that was gripping his jacket. He tried to pull free but the flowing fingers were on tight. He struggled out of the jacket and ran to the centre of the room.

The walls were moving; the plaster shifting in and out with steady rhythm, as though it was breathing. The floor was rippling, making it difficult to stand upright; the floor was shifting like the bed of the sea, shifting with the tide. He kept moving around, hoping to stay safe by movement. The ceiling cracked open and two hugely bloated black lips protruded, swollen and ugly; a snake tongue flicked out and he dived to the floor to avoid it. The ceiling retracted and he looked up into a starless night sky, velvet infinity black. Robert felt himself drawn to it; actually felt his feet leave the floor as he began to drift upwards, towards the lavish nothingness of the void.

"No!"

He screamed, a combination of voice and mind, the verbal and the imagined merged into one burst and the room reverted to normal. Before he could stand from where he had fallen a warm wind rushed over him, he heard a heartless chuckle, and the door opened and slammed shut. The room was silent.

⁂

Frank Moreland knew this was the end; his strength had been taken in capturing and holding Michael at bay, and in sending out his cries for help.

The black cloud filled his head, and there was no room left for Frank's thoughts. His head ached with the pain of his efforts and from the constant battering from Michael's power. Frank had always known his brothers were stronger than him, which was one of the reasons he found it so hard to live with his powers.

The heat bore down on him as he lay in the pit, curled like a torn piece of rope. A guard had just thrown a bucket of foul smelling liquid down on him, and he was trying to breathe without swallowing any of it. His head ached from the relentless glare of the midday sun, and somewhere in the distance a man was screaming. Then they came for him.

The top of the pit crowded with grinning yellow faces and at first he welcomed the way they blocked out the sun. Then he remembered the hut; he kicked and shouted as they dragged him from the pit, rifle butts and boots cracking ribs. Anything was better than being shown the inside of that hut.

They spat on him as they pulled him through the dust; the two men holding his feet deliberately moving apart as they pulled him, so that the pain was unbearable. Another guard prodded his groin with the bayonet fixed to his rifle and they all laughed.

The bamboo hut was getting nearer and he was getting hysterical. They opened the door and pushed him inside. Somewhere in a corner a man whimpered, another cried like a baby, one babbled like a madman. Slowly Frank's eyes grew accustomed to the gloom and he realised he was inside a torture chamber. An arm lay discarded on a table, the fingers reaching into the air as if groping for hope. One man in the tatters of a military uniform was pinned to the wall with bayonets through his hands and feet; his penis and testicles burned black by fire. Another was trussed up in a tiny cage hung from the ceiling; his eyes kept open by sliver of bamboo under the eyelids. On the floor in the corner a naked soldier was covered in black ants; they were eating the sweet syrup that covered his body.

Light flooded the room as the door opened and a tall white-faced man entered. The guards stood and bowed, but the man ignored them, turning instead to Frank. The twin blue eyes mocked him now as they had when they were boys growing up in such different directions. It was Michael and for a moment Frank felt relief but then he remembered.

A gun was held loosely in Michael's fingers.

"You were never going to amount to anything, Frank, we all knew that."

He raised the gun, pressed it into Frank's forehead and fired.

⁂

Robert saw the blood spurt from Frank's nose, mouth and ears, and knew that he had succumbed to Michael's strength. The warm wind had left the room, and Robert and Frank were alone for a few moments.

Robert closed the staring eyes, and tried to say some words that might comfort his brother on his final journey. In death Frank looked at ease, and Robert said a prayer of thanks to him for holding Michael for so long. He only hoped that with Julia and Fields, he would be able to stop the creature that Michael had become.

Julia lay in the bathtub, eyes closed, her mind relaxing after the numerous tests she had been subjected to. She had spent the afternoon with Chris Fields, but left as he poured his fifth Jack Daniels, deciding he was best laying his own ghosts to rest.

She moved her legs and felt the sensation of the warm water against her skin. She had filled the bath with scented oil and the velvet smoothness caressed her throat and chin. Starting to become drowsy, eyelids heavy, tension flowing from her body. Her limbs heavy too, muscles melting in the womblike softness of the sensual water. Was the water getting warmer?

She opened her eyes to see if the hot tap was still on, but it was closed. The room was full of steam, filling the entire room, clouding the mirror, obscuring the window. She could barely make out the end of the bath, the thick fog shrouding trails of grey movement.

The water in the bath was still getting warmer, starting to get uncomfortable. She knelt up in the bath and felt for the taps, but both were shut off and wouldn't turn. She tried to stand – maybe if she opened the window or the door the steam would evaporate – it was so thick, a sea mist rolling drunkenly and threateningly over and around her. She had trouble standing; her feet kept slipping on the bottom of the bath, as though it was covered in grease. The water was getting too hot now, starting to burn her legs. She crouched at the side of the bath, trying to raise herself up by the edges, but they were slippery as well, and her hands kept slipping.

Every time she tried to stand her feet or her hands slid off the sides of the bath and she fell back into the water.

It felt slimy, starting to stick to her skin, not like water at all; it was too thick, too sticky. It felt like soup, and it was getting hotter all the time; it was starting to scald her skin. She began to feel the rising panic; this is ridiculous – I can't get out of my bath.

Then she heard the breathing. Blinded by clouds of steam, helpless in the burning water, nakedly vulnerable, and she could hear breathing in the room with her. Low, deep rasping breathing.

She reached out, stretched her arm as far as she could, reaching for a towel. Her hand touched something that yielded as a slug would, and which shrank back from her touch. She screamed, shouted for Fields, who was in the adjoining bungalow.

There was a sickly sweet smell in the room, like over-ripe fruit. The breathing was getting stronger. A throbbing started in her head but she struggled to her feet, slipping and sliding, pushing against the walls for support. She reached down and pulled out the bath plug. The water level stayed the same. The water was bubbling now, near to boiling, and the pain was unbearable. It was as if she was standing in hot syrup, the fog beginning to choke her, and it was getting darker, the clouds of steam turning black.

'You're an attractive man, Lewis.'

'Give us the money.'

'Don't drink the milk.'

It felt as if tiny insects were crawling over her feet, and she lifted first one foot then the other, but the feeling persisted. The steam was getting thicker, the breathing getting closer.

⁂

Chris Fields poured another two fingers of Jack Daniels, aware he had had a handful too many but past caring. He was promising himself he was getting the next plane out to

Vegas, leave them wanting more, leave them to sort out their own problems.

He got up from the end of his bed, went over to the refrigerator and opened the door. Water poured all over the floor; the ice had melted, everything in there had thawed, the food rotted.

Fields looked at the table where he had left the bottle and glass; they were vibrating. The bottle cracked and broke into fragments onto the carpet. There were maggots in the glass he had been drinking from.

He looked around the room; there was mould on the carpets, the bed was covered in tendrils of green fungus. Something dropped onto his head, he brushed it off, a cockroach, he stepped on it with his heel. When he looked up at the ceiling it was crawling with insects; cockroaches, beetles, creeping and crawling over each other. Something brushed his feet; he saw spiders covering the whole floor, brown, black, large, small. They scuttled, a seething mass of them.

The bed was full of snakes; huge pythons, coiled rattlesnakes, cobras, curled and slithering in furious, quivering smoothness.

Fields tried to run, fell, and lay on the bed.

⁂

There was a woman in a bath and there were fish all around her. It was Nicole Norris and she was soaping her soft dark skin, breasts full, succulent, the nipples distended, black and angry, long and firm. Her eyes were closed and she was smoothing the soap into her skin with slow deliberate strokes.

"Place is like a maze." Bob Keating came into the room, he was naked and erect. "Hey, sugar, come and play with Uncle Bob." He had two coffees and a bag of doughnuts in his hand.

Nicole opened her eyes; they were bright blue, no pupils, just blue inviting waves. She reached her hand out of the water and grasped him. She placed him in her mouth, and bit down hard until her mouth filled with warm blood.

Keating screamed and smashed his fist into her face; her nose cracked, her teeth shattered. He pushed her under the water, her eyes open wide, brown and crying out for help. He held her under water until her struggles weakened and became merely memories.

The door burst open, and the room filled with a thick cloying smoke. Ray Norris was standing there.

"There's Frank Moreland's files; get reading."

He threw the head of a German shepherd dog at Keating; blood dribbled from the neck where it had been severed from the body. In his left hand Norris held a butcher's knife stolen from the kitchen. With a single swipe of the knife he cut off Keating's head, before arranging the dog's head on Keating's shoulders.

Norris knelt on the floor, took the knife in both hands, placed it against his stomach and pushed hard.

⁂

The office Whitney occupied was large and spacious, the desk expansive and covered with the executive equipment he felt a person in his position should have. There was a heavy quartz paperweight on the edge of the desk.

The door to his office opened and closed. In the doorway was his mother. She was naked, smiling, warm and friendly and she was inviting him to join her, beckoning to him slowly and seductively.

'You want her, Walt; you always have.'

She was coming towards him, her breasts were slippery with oil and she caressed them as she moved, rubbing the nipples with her fingers. Her pubic mound was shaved, the darkly shadowed entrance inviting him away from the terrors.

When she reached the desk she picked up the paperweight. She brought it pounding down and the side of his head cracked open like an egg thrown at a wall. She brought the weight down again and again until his face was gone and his brain trickled over the executive desk.

"Party seems to be going well!" she screamed as she ran from the room into the corridor outside. A guard challenged her to stop but she ran directly to him, launched herself at him, her outstretched fingers connecting his face. The two entwined bodies fell in a heap to the floor.

A second guard, hearing the struggle, appeared in the corridor. The woman lifted herself from the now still form of the guard, blood dripping from her lips. She cried out, as the guard raised his automatic rifle and pointed it at her. She ran towards him screaming and a single burst of automatic fire cut the woman in two.

Two guards ran into the crowded cinema room and sprayed the audience with bullets. Those that staggered out alive they attacked with machetes. All the while the guards were calling, "Nevermore."

Men and women copulated in the corridors; until guards and assistants coming across them beat them to death with anything they could lay their hands on.

A guard on the front gate went down on all fours and began attacking his colleagues with his teeth. A pack of foam-mouthed guard dogs savaged him and left him to die.

A medical assistant pulled one of the female assistants into a corner of the lab and knocked her out with the handset of a telephone. Using a scalpel he slit open her clothing, removed it all, then surgically and skilfully removed her skin. He cut round and removed her lips and eyes, placing them neatly on the folded heap of flesh and clothes. Then he raped her.

Zoë and Daniel lay motionless in bed. Daniel was awake looking down at the sleeping girl.

His mind was filled with a surfeit of emotions. Guilt tormented him; still mourning Imogen he had fallen into bed with a stranger he had met less than twenty-four hours ago. The thoughts he had dismissed about behaviour after funerals had come true for him and he didn't know how to handle them. He had rarely, if ever, had one-night stands, and here he was naked, and replete after not giving a thought about Imogen as he abandoned himself.

Zoë seemed to be sleeping but she wasn't.

He had been surprised how desperate his needs had been, and he had performed athletically as if he had a point to prove. The bruises on his body urged him on, as the point he proved was perhaps that he was still alive; no matter how guilty he felt about it, he was alive, and she was dead.

Zoë had an itch in her head, like tiny insects crawling across her brain. Daniel started to stroke her forehead very gently; but the more he stroked her head the more the sullen tension built up in her. Stroke; the muscles in her throat tensed. Stroke; the leg muscles bunched, ready to kick out. Stroke, and the insects in her head scurried away into the shadows.

Her hand was hanging loosely out of the bed. As her forehead was stroked so she was stroking a long bladed knife by the side of the bed. Stroke; she felt the sharp blade. Stroke; she felt the weight of the handle. Stroke, and she felt the pointed end.

Suddenly the tension was too much to bear and she opened her eyes, sat upright in bed and screamed.

"What's wrong?" Daniel tried to hold her, but she was shaking uncontrollably.

Slowly she succumbed to his calm, and folded herself in his arms. "Just a bad dream," she said.

"Maybe you could do with a drink?"

She struggled out of his embrace. "Good idea. I'll get them." She swung her legs out of bed, glanced down for the knife she had been stroking; it was her shoe.

"I'll have a quick shower, if that's all right?" Daniel said.

He went through into the bathroom, got into the shower, and began to shower. The water was hot, and he relaxed, the steam making him feel drowsy. He washed vigorously, feeling good. His restricted vision could just about recognise a shape outside the shower curtain. He stopped washing and waited. The water cascaded off his body; he could hear his own breathing above the jet of water. The shape came back. The curtain was ripped back and Imogen got in with him. Already naked, she wrapped her arms around him. Her tongue darted over him, echoes of past love making exciting and tantalising him. As soon as she had materialised so she seemed to disappear, and the water soon ran cold.

Drying himself Daniel lay on the bed.

In the kitchen Zoë prepared sandwiches to go with the coffee. The knife she used was long and sharp and pointed. It cut the bread easily. When she was finished she put the food and coffee on a tray; she put the knife on the tray as well. Her eyes were blank, her movements automatic.

She walked into the bedroom where Daniel smiled at her from the bed. Zoë handed him one of the empty cups, and he held it up to her so she could pour his coffee from the jug. She started to pour coffee into his cup, then moved her hand so that she was pouring it directly into his face. He screamed as the scalding liquid burned his eyes and skin. He brought his hands up instinctively to protect himself but Zoë smacked him hard on the head with the coffee jug. He fell back with blood slipping from his lip.

Zoë took the knife from the tray and pushed everything else away. She climbed onto the bed and straddled Daniel so that his arms were pinned against his sides. She placed the knife at his throat.

Daniel managed to open one eye. He could see Zoë; she was smiling sweetly.

"Trapped?"

She leaned forward on the knife and thrust it through his neck, into the pillow beneath. His blood spurted into her face. Calmly she pulled the knife out and wiped it on her leg.

She got off the limp body and stood from the bed. She tore at anything she could reach with the knife. She ripped curtains, tore the bedclothes, raked the carpet, slashed the wallpaper.

She turned to Daniel's body. She slit it open from chest to groin, and tiny white maggots spilled out. It was as if someone had slapped her round the face. The spell was broken and she recoiled in horror from the savaged body.

The maggots flopped onto the floor and she hit out at them with the knife. She seemed surprised to find the knife in her hand. She turned it on herself, cutting her wrists, slicing her skin until the blood flowed like water.

⁂

Robert Moreland was in the canteen. He sat at one of the tables, the surface of it was covered in tomato sauce, an ironic parody of the blood he knew had been spilled. He threw his mind around the centre as if it was in a pinball machine, but there was nothing there. Wait, he thought he could detect . . . a faint pulse, in one of the bungalows.

The door to Field's bungalow was open, and Robert went in. Fields was curled in the foetal position on the carpet, his arms wrapped around his head.

Robert knelt beside him and touched his shoulder.

"Get them off me," Fields pleaded. "Don't let them get me."

Robert shook him. "Chris, it's all right. There's nothing here."

Eventually, Fields began to calm, and Robert tried placing words directly into his thoughts.

'I need your help. We may be the only ones left.'

At first Fields seemed confused; he put his hands either side of his head as if he wanted to pull the words out. Then he realised who was talking to him.

"Julia is next door." His eyes darted around the room as he spoke. He was still uncertain if he was safe in there or not.

⁂

Julia opened the door wrapped in a huge towel. Fluff from the towel was stuck to her skin, red and sticky.

"Are you all right?" Fields asked.

She leaned forward and brushed a cockroach from his shoulder. "Same as you I would guess."

'Shaken not stirred.'

Julia smiled grimly as the words inserted themselves into her mind. Fields wasn't quite adept at it yet and the sensation tickled.

Robert was searching the bungalow ensuring they were alone. When he was satisfied they were he said. "There may be just the three of left. That may be what he intended."

"Or maybe we were too strong for him." Fields suggested.

Robert shook his head. "Together we can only hope we are, but separately . . . I think he was so busy with everything . . . everybody else, that we were occupied until he came back for us."

As best he could he had explained his theory about Frank holding Michael; about Michael's transformation; and about why they were all called here. He didn't believe either of them fully understood what he was saying, and they certainly didn't appreciate the possibilities of what Michael had become, or why.

Julia sat on a chair, and absent-mindedly rubbed her hair with the towel. "Is everyone else dead?" She sounded like a child learning Santa Claus didn't exist.

⁂

An extensive search of the centre had found no one else alive. More in hope than true expectancy they had come to Zoë's bungalow. She had been the last one seen with Daniel.

"There are no lights on." Julia observed.

Fields tried the door. "Locked."

They stood in the still night, wondering what to do, but the dark sky gave no answers; clouds scudded across, sheltering the pale dead face of the moon, hiding the stars that sparkled like sequins on a forgotten actress.

"I'll try around the back," Fields said. "Maybe there's a window open."

Julia touched his arm. The gesture said to be careful.

It was only after he had disappeared from their sight that they heard the scream.

Robert tried to force the door but it was solid. The screams got louder. Then they heard the laughter; almost like the laughter of the audience at a theatre or TV show; laughing at the entertainment being provided for their amusement. There was the light tinkling, piano key laughter of a group of young women, the belly laugh of men, using the comedy to release their pent up emotions. Above all the voices they could hear a bass rumbling sound like a huge beast laughing.

Lights in the bungalow began to flash on and off, strobe lighting or camera flashes in sequence. They heard wood splitting; cracking noises as if furniture was being splintered. The laughter persisted but other noises were mingled there as well; nightmare noises that might come from deformed mouths of creatures that live below the ground, fractured noises that bore no relation to human sound.

Then there was silence; and that was so much worse.

Robert beckoned Julia to stay where she was and he cautiously edged into the bungalow.

All the furniture was smashed into tiny pieces, and there was blood everywhere. The centre light was swinging from side to side, creating shifting shadows in the corners of the room.

Zoë was spread-eagled on the floor amidst the debris, part of the damage. There was a broken table lamp between her legs, the end forced inside her. It was still switched on, and occasionally her body jolted in a mockery of movement as an electric current passed through her. Her breasts were torn off; a lighted candle was stuck into her mouth, her eyes hung down her cheeks on thin threads.

Daniel was curled beside her, a large crucifix poking from his anus. His genitals had been cut off, and dangled from his mouth. His fingers had been skilfully removed and placed on his chest in a random pattern.

The room was charred from immense heat; there were hoof prints on the floor, and claw marks on the walls; teeth marks on both bodies.

"What the . . . " Fields had got in through a back window.

Suddenly the bungalow started to shake.

"It's still here," Robert shouted. "Get out quickly."

Daniel moved on the floor. Zoë was writhing in sexual ecstasy, pushing the broken lamp in and out of her vagina with increasing speed. She was sucking on the candle, wax dripping onto her face like scattered semen; moaning softly as though in the throes of orgasm.

The bungalow was vibrating violently, making it difficult to get to the door.

Daniel straddled Zoë, and began to move in rhythm with her. Robert pushed his thoughts into both their minds; they were both quite dead.

Robert got Julia and Fields out as the walls began to crack. There was a huge explosion, and tiles fell from the roof, smoke bellowing from the windows. There was a burst of light and the bungalow imploded; falling in on itself in a rush of smoke and dust.

After the noise subsided the silence of the night seemed to mock them with false serenity.

"What are we going to do?" Julia asked wearily.

"We get out of here, that's what." Fields was adamant.

Robert swept his mind through the research centre; there were many responses, but he knew they were all one. They were all Michael playing games as he had always done; only this time they weren't children playing pretend dare or die.

Fields stood in front of Robert. "Look. Maybe we were called here, or whatever, but the truth is she's exhausted." He indicated Julia, who was slouched on the ground. "And I'm no better. Everyone else is dead, for Christ's sake. I'm no hero. Let's get out of here."

Robert nodded his head. "You can try, but I doubt we can." He put his arms around Julia to try to comfort her. She felt soft and scared; he immediately thought of Rebecca and his last remaining fund of strength dissolved.

"Let's try that jeep." He pointed firmly enough but his voice trembled.

The jeep wouldn't start. They ran to another by a side gate but that wouldn't start either.

"There must be others." Julia was aware her voice was pleading.

"They'll all be dead as well," Fields admitted. "We'll have to walk."

"All the way to the city?"

"Let's just get out of here."

As they reached the gate they looked back at the research centre's buildings. The lights went out as if someone had been waiting for them to look. Fields swore under his breath and turned to the gate, but Robert held his arm. "I think the fence might be electrified."

"Surely all the power is cut off?"

Robert pointed to a line of dead animals arranged almost deliberately along the perimeter of the wire fence. He took off his shoe and threw it at the fence; there was a flash of blue light and a crackling that deafened for a moment.

"It's getting cold. Does anyone else think it's getting cold?" Julia asked.

For a while they stood looking through the gates to a freedom that was a tantalising glimpse away. Robert took control. "There's no point standing out here. Let's get back inside, see if we can rig up a generator for heat and light; maybe get a telephone or radio to work."

They re-entered the darkened centre, their footsteps echoing around the cold corridors, their words spoken in hushed whispers. They tried various telephones but none of them worked; they tried e-mail, fax, but nothing worked – they were cut off.

Working as a team, using their mind powers under Robert's guidance, they rigged a makeshift generator in the canteen, and arranged some lighting, and got a cooker to work.

While Fields and Julia cooked, Robert told them again the history he had with Michael, the entity he believed his brother had become, and he coached them in the use of their own powers, and how they could use them as a team.

⁂

Francine Fields pulled the blue gown over her head and smoothed out the lines.

"How does it look, Chris?"

Chris Fields glanced away from his own reflection in the vanity mirror and grunted an incomprehensible reply. He had married Francine three years earlier and she always looked good, that was one of the reasons he had married her.

⁂

They were dressing for a Beverley Hills party. Fields was thirty, and getting nowhere; a bit part actor on TV, a few commercials, a part time comic in the local clubs. His dreams of success were floundering and he was getting desperate. Tonight's party was a big chance; there were important people there and he needed to impress them.

"Why did we have to hire a limousine, Chris? What's wrong with our car?"

"Ours? Be serious. It's all image, Fran. I can walk home on stilts or on hand and knee but I need to arrive in style. You can only arrive once, and the important thing is for the big people to see me arrive."

"Me? It's always 'me'. What happened to 'us'?"

"It's a tough business I'm in, baby, and I have to be tough to win. What have you ever done for my career? Tonight could be my big chance to meet the right people."

Francine started to cry. "That's unfair; my job pays the rent."

"Secretarial work!"

"A steady nine to five, Chris. It buys the food, keeps us going."

Fields stood and placed his hands on her shoulders. He didn't want her spoiling her looks for the party by crying. Francine sniffed back the tears and re-applied some make-up. Fields let her go and stood in front of his mirror again; he looked good.

The party was well under way as the limousine dropped them off. The arrival was everything he'd hoped for. As they walked up the marble steps, coloured fountains playing on either side, music from the Hollywood mansion washed over them. People were seated on the steps and Fields waved and called to them; false familiar friends.

"Who was that?" Francine asked as Fields called out 'hello' to yet another stranger.

"Who knows? As long as they remember the face they may do me some good later."

The party spread through the mansion; there was wild laughter, naked couples jumping or being thrown into the pool. A bar curved around the entire side of the main room, and every imaginable drink was available. Busy too were the smaller tables laid out with discreet but openly available bowls of powder and pills.

Everyone was there, each putting on an Oscar act; smiles, more smiles, cleavages flashing, uplifts, tucks, rebuilds. Here was the community of the beautiful, and the more expensive the more well regarded the job. Francine felt ill at ease, but Fields hopped from foot to foot, feeling the atmosphere and loving it, oblivious to his wife's discomfort. Here was his opportunity, his chance to join the club, the select few . . . over by the terrace window, if he wasn't mistaken . . . yes; it was Larry Brock, the agent who handled some of the biggest comedy names in the business. Fields steered Francine in his direction.

"Mr Brock? How are you, nice to see you."

Brock was a small man with black bushy hair, an expensive tan, and a suit that was even more expensive. He turned tired cold eyes onto Fields. "Do I know you?" His voice was almost devoid of his native Bronx accent.

"Mr Brock, it's a pleasure. Chris Fields. My wife, Francine, isn't she gorgeous?"

Francine nervously held out her hand to the man. Brock looked her up and down, caressing her breasts with his eyes, a spark of interest rubbing away his natural veneer of boredom. "Charmed," he murmured.

Francine smiled at Brock. He seemed a little shy, though Chris hadn't noticed, which was typical of him. He went on talking; nervous she supposed. Then she realised Brock was still holding her hand; that was nice.

Fields had seen the way Brock looked at Francine, and the way he was still holding onto her hand. There was an angle here; something he could use. "Is your wife here, Brocky?" Brock immediately dropped Francine's hand.

"She couldn't make it tonight, I'm afraid. Visiting her mother in Tulsa."

"Too bad. Here, let me get you another drink."

As Chris wandered off, Brock took Francine's hand again. "Noisy man your husband."

"He means well," Francine said. "He's a comic and he wants to hit it big."

"They all do. Is he any good?" Brock had let his hand drop against her leg and he was stroking her. "Don't be shy, Francine. You're a lovely lady, and I don't think your husband appreciates you."

Francine couldn't help be flattered by Brock's direct approach. Chris was obviously impressed with him; perhaps she could do something to help his career after all. Maybe if she played along with Brock it might work to Chris's advantage.

Fields had no intention of returning with drinks; he thought he would leave the two of them together to see what developed. Besides there were plenty of other people at the party who might be able to help his career; he just had to meet them.

The party moved on; when it was time to leave Francine looked around for Chris but she couldn't find him. She started to get angry. Brock asked her what was wrong and offered to take her home; especially as he confided, untruthfully, that he thought he had seen Fields leave with that redhead from the game-show about an hour or two back. Perhaps he was just giving her a lift home and would come back for Francine?

Francine had been drinking all night, and now she began to drink some more. She could easily believe that Chris had gone off with some woman; it wouldn't be the first time. The drunker she got the more outrageously she flirted with Brock.

They collected their coats and left.

Next morning at seven, Fields rang Brock's home. The 'phone rang and rang; he could imagine Brock and Francine lying in a huge bed, an empty bottle on the floor . . . the ringing stopped. It was Brock.

"Who the . . . "

"Brocky. Chris Fields here."

"Who? Oh . . . "

"Can I speak to my wife, please?"

"I think you're making a mistake."

"You had a good time, Brocky? Your own wife away so you borrow mine. No problem."

"My wife . . . a divorce would ruin . . . "

"As I said, Brock, no problem. I think we can do a deal here."

"A deal . . . sure, clubs, contracts. You want work, don't you?"

"Send my wife home, Brocky, and we can talk tonight. I want the big time, and you are my passport there."

"You've got talent, Fields, I'm sure; you'll go all the way."

"I intend to."

Francine arrived home later that morning; tired and guilty. Nothing Fields wanted was too much trouble for her; he became more and more unreasonable but she didn't mind. He never once asked her where she had spent the night of the party. She was surprised when he told her a few days later that Brock was taking him on as a client; and she was embarrassed when Brock began to visit their house but gradually Fields begun to hit big. The clubs got bigger and richer, there were TV slots, an album a series, talk of feature films. They moved house to a bigger place.

Suddenly he was one of the top five comedy names in the country. He dropped Brock when another agent, Marty Fontaine, bigger and with a better offer, came along. It had taken five years but it was the moment Brock had waited for. He rang Francine when he knew Fields wouldn't be there and told her all about the deal that had been made. Described how Francine had been used.

When Fields came home that night Francine was waiting for him.

"Is it true?" She knew of course that it was.

Fields laughed. "Sure it's true. I got what I wanted, and you did all right out of it too."

"You used me!"

"I prostitute myself every time I go on stage; with my talent I just needed the break. You were it."

She spat at him and he slapped her across the face. He grabbed his jacket and left the house. When he returned Francine was lying on the bed, a bottle and some pills next to her. The note said 'I loved you once, but you only loved yourself. I'm sorry about that.'

He burned the note, called the police, and enjoyed his success.

⁂

The intimate atmosphere created by Fields reminiscences was beginning to get claustrophobic. The canteen was eerily silent save for the low chugging of the generator. The light it gave was bright, but it flickered every so often.

Julia laid her hand over Fields'. She didn't know what to say, and Fields sensed he had made them both uncomfortable.

"I think I'll just stretch my legs in the corridor."

Robert held up his hand. "That's not a good idea."

"I just need to clear my head. Ten minutes at most; keep track of me through here." He tapped his finger to the side of his head and gave a tight smile.

After Fields left Julia and Robert sat in silence for a while.

⁂

Fields had never felt so alone. He had lived all his life with nameless fears that had induced headaches, blackouts, and those strange flashes he had grown accustomed to; but now Robert had given a name to it, and explained what it was he felt as if he was losing control over it.

The thing that seemed to be roaming the centre . . . suddenly he heard music. Perhaps Julia had found a radio that worked . . . no, the music was coming from the opposite direction to the canteen. He walked towards the music and found it was coming from the cinema room. Standing outside he could hear the music clearly; it was the kind he might hear at the clubs before he appeared on stage.

The door to the cinema opened, to reveal an interior where the rows of seats had been ripped out and now stood in clusters around tables. The chairs and tables were intimately lit, and surrounded a small dance floor. Where the screen had been was a spot lit stage. At the tables people were drinking, eating and laughing; one or two couples were smooching on the dance floor; waiters were carrying trays of drinks around.

"Would you like to dance?"

The music was getting louder. He looked at the woman who had spoken to him. It was the pretty blonde from Las Vegas, blood still staining her breasts.

"I said, 'would you like to dance?'"

He found himself leading her onto the dance floor. She danced real close to him, 'it's okay, honey', and her perfume wafted into his nostrils, heady and cloying.

"Would you like to dance?"

Fields snorted. "What do you think we're doing?"

He looked down at her pretty face but it was gone. White parchment skin, creased like tissue paper covered where her features should have been. He pushed her away and she fell to the floor, where she writhed in time with the music. The music was getting louder, but no one else seemed to notice. As he watched the woman on the floor the skin on her face began to crack, splitting open like dry earth. A black tongue protruded from the crack where her mouth should have been. Her hands were changing into grotesquely formed claws with black curving nails. Her body was swelling, the seams of her dress splitting against the pressure. Instead of pure white flesh being revealed there was black wrinkled skin, resembling very creased cloth. The parchment covering her face was gone, and beneath was a hideous mask of swollen lumps and sores. There were no eyes, but the thing was struggling to its feet, holding out its parodies of arms.

"Curtain, Mr Fields."

The words were spoken into his ear by a maroon jacketed man at his elbow who was pointing to the stage. "You're on, Mr Fielding."

"Fields. It's Fields."

The stage was brightly lit, the curtains pulled back, a stool in centre stage, highlighted by the spot, a mike standing in front. He looked for the woman but she was gone; all he could see were eager faces at tables, all waiting for him.

"Ladies and gentlemen. All the way from Las Vegas, please give it up for Chris Fieldsssssssss."

Fields found himself walking up the two steps onto the stage and the spotlight hit him between the eyes. The band quietened, the people hushed. He was on.

"Good evening ladies and . . . no don't stop that's my probably funniest. Listen I'm frightened of my entire act . . .

no, dentists, I'm scared of Mickey Mouse. Have you ever tried to get through without opening your mouth? I mean oral hygiene . . . who needs Francine? Hey, Brocky, how was she?"

"This guy's a joke, not his act."

Fields laughed into the microphone; his head was spinning, and he was hot, the sweat pouring down his back. He looked into the spotlight and it became the burning eye of the sun and he was a prisoner in a pit.

"My wife's name was Francine and I killed her. That's right I took the booze and the pills and I shoved them down her throat. I wish I had told her I loved her."

"Loved you too, Chris," a voice called from the audience.

"Fran? Is that you?"

The stage descended into darkness as all the lights went out. Fight it, Fields told himself, fight it; use your power to call the others. A light flickered in the audience, a cigarette lighter. "Hold it still." It was Francine's voice.

"Fran?"

The band started to play again, a medley of Sinatra songs. He felt someone by his side; it was the blackened woman-thing. He tried to push it away but it clung to his leg. Gradually all the lights came back on and the audience was quietly going about their business, eating, drinking, having a good time.

"Hey, listen to me; I'm Chris Fields."

They all ignored him; until one by one they turned to stare at him. They all had bright blue eyes.

"Would you like to dance?" It was Francine's voice coming out of the gaping lipless mouth of the thing draped around him. He tried to push her away, and the audience started to laugh. He was screaming but the more he struggled the more they howled with laughter. Tears were rolling down some of their faces.

"Stop!" he yelled. "This isn't an act."

But they weren't listening to him.

"Ladies and gentlemen, let's hear it for an absolute jerk, a total asshole."

"No, wait I didn't mean to kill her. I'm sorry."

Then there was silence and he was looking out over a ruined cinema, bodies strewn over the rows of seats, drying blood on the floor, the screen slashed, bodies everywhere. He was alone on stage.

⁂

Julia and Robert ran into the insanity.

The bodies in the cinema were starting to twitch. The screen was showing a film. It showed a dark city street. There was no soundtrack; rubbish was strewn about, streetlights were broken, buildings on fire. The dark street was empty except for shadowed alleys where shapes moved. Along the street a little boy was walking.

"That's Matt!" Julia cried out. "That's my son."

Fields was sitting in the front row, a box of popcorn in his hand. "They're waiting for him."

On screen Matt was looking for someone in the street. A sleek black saloon car eased itself from the kerb, tyres whirring on the rain soaked street. It glided almost noiselessly, its engine purring softly like a contented cat. From behind its heavily tinted windows four pairs of eyes watched Matt.

The car began to move slowly towards the little boy.

Fields began laughing. "Who's in the car? This is better than the late, late show."

The bodies on the floor, strewn over the seats, were rising; moving as a group towards Fields.

On screen the car pulled up level with Matt. One window slid down and an arm reached out from within; a long slim arm, naked but for a diamond bracelet that glittered in the moonlight. In the elegant hand was a plastic toy ray gun. Matt saw it and his eyes lit up with excitement.

"Don't take it, Matt!" Julia yelled. "Don't take it."

Matt walked to the black car, and reached for the gun. Other hands from within grabbed him, and he was lifted inside. Suddenly the sound system turned on and the soundtrack blared out; screams of pain, of bone being scraped.

Julia rushed to the screen and began tearing at it with her hands. Trying to shut out the horror and the noise.

Fields screamed; he was surrounded by dead bodies; some standing, others crawling, all reaching out to him, scratching at his clothes, pulling at his arms and legs.

Robert ran to help him, but Fields pushed him away. "Get away, this is *my* audience. Did you hear about the guy took an overdose? Pretty hard to swallow I know . . . "

Robert closed his eyes and probed into Fields' brain. There were dozens of responses; confused, terrified, angry.

Julia was slumped in front of the cinema screen. Robert sent a message to her. *'Help me get Fields out of here.'* She seemed to notice the dead people for the first time. They were crowding Fields and Robert against the far wall. Julia drew up a strong electrical charge in her mind and released it around the room. She saw Fields and Robert both flinch but it worked; the bodies of the dead reacted violently, some bending in two with the shock, others fell shaking to the floor.

'Come on, let's get out.'

Between the three of them they worked their way into the corridor, but it was in total darkness.

"The generator must have failed." Robert said.

They moved slowly along the corridor, stopping when they got to a door.

'What's inside there?'

'Keep going.'

Fields had been silent since they had left the cinema. Now he said. "This smells funny."

Julia waited for the punch line but Robert sniffed the air. "He's right. It smells like smoke."

Fields started to mumble in a W C Fields voice. " . . . never give a sucker an even break . . . on the whole I'd rather be in Philadelphia . . . Rebecca was a great fuck, Robert."

The lights came on, and the corridor was bathed in brilliant white light. They saw that the end they had been walking towards was bricked up; red building bricks had been erected across the height and width, completely blocking off the route. All the doors had been boarded up; planks nailed across them.

The only option was to go back they way they had come; they turned behind them and saw that the corridor reached into a seemingly endless infinity. There was no door at the end, there was no end wall; the side walls stretched so far ahead that they lost sight of them. It was like looking into a vast tunnel.

"Marty, heh, Marty Fontaine." Fields pulled away from them. He could see someone coming towards him. "Marty, this is a pretty lousy gig you got me here. Still as Moses said 'Keep taking the tablets.'"

Robert looked at Julia. *'Help me.'*

'He's resisting.'

Fields walked further into the tunnel. "Heh, Marty, did you hear about the nun and the priest went into the desert on two camels?"

A figure was forming ahead of Fields, the figure of a man. Smoke swelled around him, black smoke, thick and oily. From the tunnel behind the figure was the sound of baying dogs; on the tunnel ceiling were bats hanging lifeless.

"So she says 'In that case forget about me, and stick it in the camel.'"

The figure was fully formed now; half man, half beast; huge, towering, with arms hanging limp and long, coarse black hair covering the bulk of the body, yellow jagged fangs, talons glinting in the full glare of the light. The eyes were the most obviously human element – blue, bright madly shining blue.

Field saw only his agent, "Marty."

The monster spoke to him in Fontaine's voice. "You're all washed up, Chris. Finished. You were always second rate for me, I'm glad to ditch you."

"Marty, you can't do this. I thought we were friends."

"The only friend you ever had was Francine, and see how you treated her."

The figure approached Fields, moving faster, and faster. Fields was beginning to realise this was wrong; this wasn't Marty.

The figure glided over the slime-covered floor; blue plasma drifted out behind it, billowing blue mist. The figure slammed straight into Fields and soaked right into him; the mist trailed on behind and was swallowed by Fields body. Fields seemed to swell; like a balloon filled with water his skin stretched and whatever was inside him was pushed outwards. He dropped to his knees, turned and faced the others. His eyes were blank, nothing there, and his mouth was hanging open, spittle dribbling from the corners. His skin was bloated, stretched to capacity. He stood and began to walk; looking like a beached whale, flopping helplessly.

The bloated obscenity was filling the tunnel entrance. Illuminated by the light, the skin was stretching still further, the veins stood out clearly, the skin almost transparent. Then the pressure from within got too great, and the skin began to split. Black liquid oozed out, dripping from the eyes, the ears, then the chest, and the legs. The legs gave way and Fields fell to the floor. His features were almost lost; the bloated skin had released all the black liquid and the skin hung in folds. The split edges of the skin were red raw. The body lay in a fetid pool of stinking black liquid that swelled around Julia's feet. She could feel the heat through the soles of her shoes.

'He's draining away, Robert.' The mocking voice insinuated itself into his brain.

Robert saw the body finally dissolve into the black pool.

"Mummy?"

Julia looked into the bright tunnel; it was Matt, he was beckoning to her, and he was holding a plastic toy ray gun.

'It's not Matt, Julia.'

It was too late for Robert's warning. Matt was turning back into the tunnel, and Julia was following him. Robert tried to hold her arm, and the tunnel swallowed them both.

The tunnel was dark now, the walls rough and slimy, the floor sloping this way and that, like the entrails of a huge beast.

'Where's Matt? I don't see him.'

'He's probably tucked up safe and warm at home where you left him.'

Robert probed the way back. There was a dense black cloud barring the way. The way ahead seemed easier, so they moved forward, into a chamber, slightly wider than the tunnel. There was water under their feet, and their faces brushed through cobwebs. There were two windows in the chamber; they went to the first one.

They were looking out over a wide expanse of ice; no, the more they looked they realised what they were seeing was a vast ocean of glass. Beneath the glass, faces pressed against the cold surface, and gradually they realised they were looking into the faces of everyone they had ever known. Almost everyone; there was no Rebecca, no Matt, no . . .

'What is it?' Julia asked Robert.

'Your idea of Heaven, my dear,' a deep, bass voice replied. *'Or is it?'*

The faces under the glass were screaming out in silent turmoil; agony written on each face, the eyes pleading.

The second window was smaller, and the scene darker, a little harder to focus on. Julia saw her father, he was holding Matt on his knee, but Matt was crying. Julia's father was wearing a Mickey Mouse mask, and laughing as he stroked and fondled the boy. Julia's mother appeared in the misty scene; she was carrying a small axe. Matt pointed to her and smiled. Mickey Mouse frowned and the axe was buried into his head. Blood spurted over Matt's nude body and the boy started to cry.

The scene altered and Robert watched as Rebecca took curtains down from their house in Boston. She threw them in a heap in the garden, on top of tablecloths, towels, suits, shirts. She was wearing her wedding dress. She poured something from a can over the heap and struck a match; the fire flared, licking hungrily into the evening air. Imogen ran into the scene; she began arguing with Rebecca and slapped her around the face. Rebecca responded by pushing Imogen into the fire.

The window started to cloud over.

"There's something coming down the tunnel." Robert said.

'My idea of hell,' the deep voice chuckled.

There was the sound of dogs in a hunting pack, barking and growling; and in amongst them was the sound of whistles and voices, as well as the grunts of larger animals.

Robert and Julia ran through the tunnel; there was water up to their ankles, and the noises behind them were getting louder. They turned a corner and found themselves standing in a wheat field; the ripe corn reaching up to their waists. Behind them there was no sign of the tunnel.

A pack of hunting dogs surrounded them; yellow eyes, sharp pointed, froth coated teeth. There was a low growling of blood lust in their throats.

Robert took Julia's hand and held it tight. *'Concentrate.'*

The dogs circled them, snarling warily. The pack drew together as one huge beast and pounced. Julia felt teeth sink into her leg, and felt the blood flow down her leg; but when she looked there was nothing biting her.

'Concentrate.'

*'I am hungry, Robert. Feed the beast. Let me have her, and I will let you go.'*Rebecca appeared in Robert's mind's eye. *'Let this bitch go and I can give you back your wife, Robert.'*

Robert squeezed Julia's hand and sent jolt after jolt of energy into her mind. *'Fight.'*

Julia took hold of both of Robert's hands. They faced each other and the concentration played out on their faces. A wall built around them and gradually the dogs faded away. Julia felt the pressure on her leg diminish, and watched as a single dog slinked away, cowering in defeat.

Around them the air was getting warmer. Black clouds were eddying around them; whipping into their eyes, choking their mouths. Figures danced around them, enticing and alluring; promising what they could not fulfil, telling them everything would be all right, sneaking touches inside their clothes, coating their flesh with sticky scents.

Their eyes began to smart.

'We have to get back to the tunnel,' Julia pleaded.

'No. We have to defeat this first.'

Then Michael was standing in front of them; the Michael from Robert's memory. Michael as a young man, his features already sullied with the thoughts he was carrying in his head.

Robert locked minds with Michael and they fought. Julia was a helpless onlooker as the brothers probed and pushed; waves of energy sparking off them. Gradually, when Robert was fully stretched, his powers pulled to their limits, Michael began to change shape. The young adult began to adopt the guise of the beast; the bargain he had struck took hold in the folds of skin that drooped from his frame. The hair grew thick and coarse; the tentacles flopped out, the huge swollen head rolled dangerously.

Julia sensed that Robert could do no more; he was barely holding Michael and there could only be one conclusion. She moved away from them and let her mind probe back and around. One by one she detected them, and she called them.

Michael was battering Robert's defences and there was little Robert could do to resist. He had always known his brother had stronger powers but only now did he realise how developed those powers were.

Then the band of pressure in his subconscious mind began to loosen. He was able to push back and feel Michael retreat. Robert risked opening his eyes and what he saw gave him the strength to push hard. The huge creature was shrinking; the body falling back to the young Michael. The reason was that Julia was conducting dozens of people surrounding him. There was Daniel, Rebecca, Whitney, and others Robert didn't recognise. Julia was instructing them to direct their feelings of hate and anger directly at the heart of the beast. That it was working was evident, as the figure of Michael was beginning to fade; the skin translucent, almost diaphanous. Then it had gone completely.

Julia opened her eyes and Robert hugged her. They were in the canteen in the research centre.

Robert probed but couldn't detect anything.

'I assure you my hell is much more pleasant than any you can imagine.' Julia smiled as she inserted the words into Robert's mind.

He slapped her around the face. She held her head in her hands and cried. After a while she stopped, and Robert took her hands in his. Tentatively he explored her thoughts.

He believed they were now completely alone.

Biography: Len Maynard and Mick Sims

By the end of 2002 Len Maynard & Mick Sims will have been responsible for 40 books in the genre. Details can be found at www.maynard-sims.com. Active Horror Writers Association members, their two hardback collections, **Shadows At Midnight**, 1979 and 1999, and **Echoes Of Darkness**, 2000, will be followed in 2002 by their third collection, **Incantations**, published by **prime books** USA. These books and stories from them have gained Stoker recommendations and Honourable Mentions, and numerous other stories have also been published in a variety of anthologies and magazines. Their standalone novella **The Hidden Language Of Demons** is out in 2002 from **prime**, USA. 2001 saw **Moths**, their novella, available in USA, as well as two collections of their stories, essays and interviews each containing 100,000 words – **The Secret Geography Of Nightmare** and **Selling Dark Miracles** – one introduced by Hugh Lamb and the other by Stephen Jones, all three from **Cosmos Books** USA. Their fourth collection, **Falling Into Heaven**, is completed, as is a short novel, **The Seminar**. As editors they produce **Darkness Rising** the USA anthology series, and are editing the retrospective anthology, **Best Of Enigmatic Tales**, and an original anthology, **Cold Touch** with William Simmons. As publishers they ran **Enigmatic Press** in the UK, which produced **Enigmatic Tales**, and its sister titles. They co-edit and publish **F20** with David Howe for The British Fantasy Society. They are currently working on two novels and numerous stories.

Printed in the United States
3138